SINGAPORE GOLD

A TALE OF JUST REWARD

Lt. Kincaid

1941

LANCE STOUFFER

A *TOSA* files novel

HEATHROW PUBLISHING

Singapore Gold

A Tale of Just Reward

By

Lance Stouffer

A *TOSA* files novel

A Heathrow Publishing Book, Heathrow, Florida

www.HeathrowPublishing.com

Cover designed by Brian E. Bourke

ISBN-13: 978-0-615-58900-8

To all those Australian, British, Indian and Malaysian men and women who served in the Singapore and Malaysia theatre of war during World War II. We salute your service and memory,

And,

To Jack for a thousand reasons we won't discuss here!

Sometimes we must listen to the echoes from the past and act to make things right!

PART ONE

Chapter 1 – Singapore, January 30, 1942, Malaya Command
Headquarters, 2 pm

Singapore had been under day and night bombing siege from
the air by the Japanese 3rd Air Division of the 25th Japanese
Army for almost a month when Lt. Gerald R. Kincaid of the
Australian 8th Division, on returning that morning with a
convoy from Malaya to resupply, was ordered unexpectedly to
Malaya Command Headquarters at Fort Canning. Apprehensive,
he wondered what all this was about, not knowing that an
extraordinary adventure and his worst nightmare was about to
begin. They sent a staff car to fetch him from the supply depot,
which was even more curious as he was only an artillery
lieutenant. The driver, an Indian Army Sergeant, said nothing
during the journey. Maybe they want some first hand
intelligence of our defenses at Tebong Station, he thought as the
car rolled south down the main road into Singapore City. Left
and right were refugees carrying all their worldly possessions
heading in the same direction. 'I will tell them at headquarters

7

that we're getting our ass kicked by the new type of guerrilla warfare the Japanese were using to their success,' he thought to himself.

Arriving in front of the headquarters building an Indian Army private opened the car door and snapped to attention and saluted. Upon exiting the car, Kincaid returned the salute and began walking up the steps past the Indian Army sentries behind their sand bagged stations and entered the building. He walked up to the nearest desk, that of a Captain Willoby. He stopped, saluted and announced, "Lt. Kincaid reporting as ordered Sir." He held his salute until the Captain looked up from his papers and saluted back.

"Follow me Lieutenant," he said and both men began walking briskly inside the building across the marble floor their footsteps in perfect cadence. Kincaid noticed the high fever pitch of the office, with staff literally running with their papers, books and boxes on their assigned tasks. Typewriters in the background were making their unique din to add to the office bustle. They continued down a corridor to some inner offices that had two more guards, this time British soldiers in front of the door. Saluting and passing them, they entered these inner offices overlooking a central courtyard when Captain Willoby turned.

"Wait here," he said as Kincaid froze in his steps and watched Willoby stride to one of the offices. He saw the name Percivel on the door, and knew this was the 'Ole Man' in charge of the whole shebang. Why does the General want to see me, Kincaid wondered? He could see Willoby knock on the door and step inside. In an instant he returned and waved for him to enter. Kincaid stepped lively and entered the office.

"General, this is Lt. Kincaid, Australian 8th Division 2nd artillery just returned from Tebong Station for resupply,"

Willoby said as Kincaid walked forward, snapped to attention and saluted.

"Excellent," General Percivel said as he stood and saluted. "Now please leave us for a moment Captain. I'll bring him back to you shortly." With that Willoby saluted, did an about face and walked out of the office, closing the door behind him.

"Now Lieutenant, please be seated," he said gesturing to a comfortable arm chair in front of his desk. "Smoke?" he asked as he offered a cigarette from a pack on his desk to Kincaid.

"Yes Sir," he replied taking the smoke.

Kincaid reached into his pocket and pulled out a new Zippo lighter with an Australian flag painted on the top half and his name engraved in the middle. The general noticed it as he was offered, in turn, a light by Kincaid.

"Say, a pretty fancy lighter," he said as both men lit their smokes.

"Yes Sir," Kincaid replied, "a gift from my younger brother for Christmas. A yank design, but sturdy."

"Lieutenant," Percivel said, "You've been selected for a very important mission because of your map reading skills and these are your orders. I want you to take four sacks from the Hong Kong and Shanghai Bank to a shrine area, near Taman Sri Malaya on the Kota Tinggi trail, some 25 kilometers from here. Here look at this map and you'll see where you're going," as the General pointed to a map on his desk with a small 'x' drawn where he said the shrine was.

"When you get near Taman Sri, here on the map, you'll take the side road to an old shrine which is about 3 or 4 kilometers off the main road about here," he said as he continued pointing to the map.

"I want you to bury the sacks somewhere near the shrine, well hidden, and I mean that. The ground must look undisturbed when you leave. No traces that you were ever there. Are we clear?" he said.

"Yes General, I fully understand," Kincaid replied looking at the map sideways.

"Good Lieutenant, now when you bury the sacks, I want you to memorize the exact map coordinates, and use that fancy lighter of yours to burn your orders and the map. The map is very detailed with grids easily read by an artillery man like you," Percivel exclaimed.

"Now you'll need two lorries, two drivers and a four man squad to accomplish this mission and I've got Captain Willoby working on getting everything arranged now. You'll pick up the men, including Sergeant Standish from my headquarters group, at the Bukit Timah barracks within the hour. The drivers will know the roads up there, and the men will also be familiar with the area. Have you been up that way before Lieutenant?" the General asked.

"No Sir, I have not," Kincaid replied.

"Well good, not a problem, you'll do fine," Percivel said and continued, "Now Kincaid, I want you to come back here with the coordinates. And, be sure to burn this map and your orders before you head back," he said again as he handed both to him. I don't want the Japs to get their hands on them, but not to worry, they are still way northwest held up at Tebong Station as you know and at Mersing on the east side up the way you're going so you won't be in harms way at all."

Kincaid looked at the one page, single spaced typed order on Malaya Command stationary detailing what he was to do. It was signed by the general himself. Kincaid read it as fast as he could to include the last sentence in boldface type.

'TO FIELD COMMANDERS/OFFICERS
RENDER ALL ASSISTANCE TO LT. KINCAID
ON EXPEDITED PRIORITY ONE THIS
OFFICE. PERCIVEL.'

"Lieutenant, do you have any questions?" he asked.

"Yes Sir, this assignment seems a bit unusual, why me?"
Kincaid asked.

"Lieutenant, these are difficult times, and I can assure you, if
there was any other alternative right now, I would take it, but
we are cut off by air and sea right now. I will explain everything
to you on your return tomorrow morning when you bring me
the coordinates. Keep all this hush-hush, even from your men,
and ah yes, I forgot, you'll leave across the causeway at 6 pm
tonight, so you better get ready. They are expecting you at the
bank on Collyer Quay at 5 pm tonight. See Mr. Maxwell when
you get there and show him your orders. Everything's arranged.
Now I'll take you back to Captain Willoby," he said.

"General Sir," Kincaid said while standing, "are we going to
win this one?"

"Indeed," Percivel replied, "The Japs will never take fortress
Singapore if I have anything to do with it. You can take that to
the bank Lieutenant!"

Kincaid snapped to attention and followed the general
through the offices back to the desk of Captain Willoby who
stood as they approached. On arrival, Percivel turned to
Kincaid, shook his hand, and said good luck, saluted and then
walked away. Left standing in front of Willoby's desk with his
orders and map in hand, Willoby asked him to take a seat.

"Kincaid, the staff car outside will take you to Bukit Timah
barracks, where your squad and two lorries are waiting,"

Willoby said. "Make sure you have everything you need for the assignment before you leave. Good luck Lieutenant."

Kincaid stood again, saluted Capt. Willoby, turned and walked out the front door to the waiting staff car. He got in the back seat again and the car pulled away heading north and west to the Bukit Timah barracks. The same Indian Army driver again said nothing, but obviously had been told where to go by Willoby.

"Gerry old boy, what have you got yourself into," he muttered under his breath as he unfolded and looked at the map and his orders again which read:

> Malaya Command Headquarters Special Assignment: 30 January 1942: Lt. G. Kincaid, Australian 8th Division. Proceed Hong Kong and Shanghai Bank in downtown Singapore and take four sacks via lorry to designated area on the Kota Tinggi trail Malaya for disposition. Return to Singapore by morning 31 January 1942. Report this office.

He pulled out another cigarette and lit it up with his Zippo and gazed out the window at the continuing stream of refuges flooding into the city from Malaya and the bombing destruction and building fires still burning in places.

Chapter 2

In less than thirty minutes, the staff car pulled into the Bukit Timah Army barracks and proceeded to assembly building 413. The car stopped in front and the driver jumped out and opened the rear door for Kincaid. He folded the orders and map and stuffed them in his breast pocket and got out. Greeting him was Sergeant Standish, clearly of the British Army who stood at attention and saluted as Kincaid walked toward him. Returning the salute Kincaid told Standish to stand at ease.

"Sergeant, are you aware of my special mission?" he asked.

"Sir," Standish replied, "I was ordered to assemble a team for an overnight run to Malaya which I have done. I've got three Aussie Privates – Alsip, McKnight, and Perth and two drivers; one an Indian Army Corporal named Desai and the other a Malaysian irregular Corporal named Beng waiting out back. He knows the roads up there well. They said you would give us the orders when you got here."

"Right," Kincaid said, "let's see the men."

Sergeant Standish pointed around the building and they walked to the back where Kincaid could see the two lorries and his squad of men huddled in front. The sergeant shouted out '*Atten-shon*' and all snapped to attention and saluted. Kincaid approached saluting.

"At ease men and circle up." he said as he looked around at the five faces in front of him with Sergeant Standish standing to his side. "I see my three Aussie brothers here. Now who is Alsip and where are you from?"

"Sydney," Alsip replied with a big smile on his face.

"And McKnight, where are you from," he asked

"Sydney also."

"And you Perth are you from Perth?" Kincaid jokingly asked.

"No Sir, I'm from Adelaide," Perth responded.

"Well, we won't hold that against you Private," Kincaid quipped back as the men all chuckled.

"Now Corporal Desai, where is home for you?

"Near Bombay, a town called Poona" Desai responded from behind a big smile.

"And Private Beng," he asked looking at him, "where is home for you?"

"Penang," he replied.

"Are you familiar with the road to Kota Tinggi? He asked.

"Yes Sir, I have driven that road many times," Beng replied in exceptionally good English.

"Excellent, you will be my driver," Kincaid ordered.

"And you Sergeant?" he asked looking at Standish

"Sir, Liverpool," Standish replied with a grin.

"Well, a fine empire team you've assembled Sergeant," Kincaid said as the smile left his face, "now for the business at hand. Men, we've a tough priority one delivery assignment ahead and we leave here within the hour. I want shovels and torches for all and one more spare tire, and five extra 18 liter petrol flimsies for each lorry. I want each of you in jungle battle uniform with helmets. I want Sten guns and side arms for each man with triple the ammunition load and extra water and rations. And Sergeant," he said turning to Standish, "I want all this done in thirty minutes."

Sergeant Standish looked at him curiously, but took over barking orders to the men as Kincaid stepped back. Since he was already in tropical battle uniform with helmet there was nothing for him to do but watch his orders followed out. Out came another cigarette and the Zippo lighter as he planned his next move. Within thirty minutes he could see everything being assembled and put into each lorry. Two of the men came out of the assembly building carrying the Sten guns and ammunition. They were all now dressed in battle uniform. Just as thirty minutes was up, Sergeant Standish walked up, stood at attention, saluted and said all was in ready.

"Sergeant," Kincaid said after saluting, "you ride in the second lorry and follow me downtown to the Hong Kong and Shanghai bank on Collyer Quay. Keep it close."

Kincaid got into the front seat of the first lorry. Corporal Beng had already started the lorry and had it in first gear as Kincaid slammed the door. He turned and looked in the back of the lorry at Alsip and McKnight.

"You mates ready?" he asked and both replied "Yes sir."

"Corporal, head to downtown Singapore. The bank on Collyer Quay. Let's go," he said as Beng let out the clutch and the Bedford lorry leapt ahead.

It was just after 4 pm when both lorries pulled out of the Bukit Timah Barracks and headed east to downtown. The afternoon thunderstorm was just beginning and he knew this would slow them up a bit, but he was sure they could be at the bank by 5 pm. The thunderstorm passed quickly and the sun come out again to make everything extra muggy, but with the windows down this allowed something of a breeze to make it slightly less unbearable. They wound their way through the back streets of Singapore and Kincaid's adventure was moving into high gear.

Chapter **3**

Corporal Beng pulled into the narrow alley next to the Hong Kong and Shanghai Bank at just after 5 pm. It was a stately and impressive colonial building and so far had escaped the Japanese bombs. The second lorry pulled in right behind them. The streets were crowded with refugees, as was the alley.

"Wait here," he said to Beng as he opened the door and headed back to talk with Sergeant Standish, who was getting out of his lorry when Kincaid came up to him.

"Sergeant, I want your men ready when I come out of the bank, over there at that side entrance," he said pointing to the doorway.

Immediately Sergeant Standish was barking orders as Kincaid walked to the front door of the bank and tried the door. It was locked, but a uniformed guard opened the door for him. Once inside he asked where Mr. Maxwell could be found.

"That office at the end, over there." He said pointing the way. Kincaid said thanks and walked over to the office and knocked on the door.

"Come in," came the reply from within.

Kincaid opened the door and walked to the front of the desk of Mr. Maxwell and handed him his orders, signed by General Percivel.

"I'm Lt. Kincaid here for the sacks," he said as Maxwell read the orders, handed them back and asked him to accompany him. They walked out of his office and went straight to the main lift, where Maxwell pushed the down button. Soon the door opened with an attendant sitting on a stool at the controls.

"Down please," Maxwell said as the door closed and the elevator started to descend to the basement. The attendant opened the door and they stepped out and were standing in the vault anteroom. The vault door was open with two guards standing nearby, but there was a thick metal bar door just inside the vault that Maxwell strode up too and opened from a key in his possession.

Kincaid followed him into the vault and saw two sacks sitting on each of two dollies in the corner. Two other vault attendants appeared from behind him. At Maxwell's command each began wrestling the dollies forward to the vault entrance. He could see the sacks were heavy duty and made of leather and canvas with something that looked like chainmail armor covering the top and bottom 1/3. They were clearly strongboxes of the sack variety.

"Here are the sacks Lt. Kincaid," Maxwell said, "we'll help you get them up to the first floor where you'll have to sign the release."

"Mr. Maxwell," Kincaid responded, "mind telling me what's inside these sacks?"

"Do you mean they didn't tell you?" Maxwell blurted out in a rather elevated pitch.

"No Sir, my orders are just to pick up four sacks from you at 5 pm today," Kincaid said rather coolly.

"This is the Army's gold," Maxwell replied stepping up to him in a hushed tone only Kincaid could here.

"I see," Kincaid answered with his heart now racing and added, "and how much gold is that?"

"1,000 pounds dead weight to be exact," Maxwell replied, "Now let's get you on your way."

The two vault attendants strained at each cart as they pushed them toward the elevator. It took two trips to get the four sacks to the main floor. Kincaid stayed back with the second dolly as Maxwell took the first dolly to the main floor. Soon they were pushing both dollies to the side fire door on the alley where the lorries were parked. As the fire door opened, Kincaid stepped out and waived for Sergeant Standish to come over.

"Sergeant, it'll take two men to lift each sack. At a snap of his fingers privates Alsip, McKnight and Perth came forward. The first two grabbed the handle on the first sack and struggled with the 250 pounds of dead weight between them. They semi carried and dragged the sack to the first lorry. The drivers stood by the tailgate and helped them lift the sack on board. Sergeant Standish and Private Perth were straining with the second sack and everyone helped toss it into the back of the first lorry. They repeated this exercise two more times with the final two sacks and finally wrestled them into the back of the second lorry.

"Now, Lt. Kincaid, will you please sign this release?" Maxwell said as he thrust some paperwork in front of Kincaid to sign, which he did on the front fender of the Bedford.

"That's it Lieutenant," he said walking away, "good luck on your journey."

With that, Maxwell, the two attendants with dollies and the bank guard re-entered the side door of the bank, where it slammed shut.

Kincaid turned and saw all his men looking at him with that expression of 'what is going on here' and 'what's next.' He raised his hand, summoned them over and began to explain.

"Men, listen up," he said. "We're now beginning our journey to Malaya. I'll brief you all again when we clear the causeway and are on the outskirts of Johore Bahru. I want all you on your toes to protect that cargo. I want that second lorry right behind us at all times. If you have any mechanical problems honk and we'll all pull over."

Everyone got aboard their lorry and so began the slow drive north to the causeway across the Straits of Johore and into Malaya. Just as they got started air raid sirens began going off and soon the sound of explosions in the city could be heard as the Japanese Airmen were on another unopposed bombing milk run raining death on Singapore the third time that day. Kincaid had heard rumors that over 1,000 were killed each day from the bombing. Looking out the window at the steady stream of refugees on both sides of the road heading into the city he knew it would only get worse. The two lorries slowly worked their way north retracing their journey west on the Bukit Timah Rd and then north on Woodlands Road toward the causeway. The highway was clogged with other lorries and troops heading in both directions. They passed thousands of British, Australian, Indian and Malayan troops heading south. Their faces each told the same story that something was not right. Kincaid knew first hand things were not quite right and wondered how General Percivel could be so upbeat and yet these front line boys were so down.

Chapter **4**

Approaching the Johore causeway, Kincaid's two lorries were stopped dead due to a monumental traffic jam. There was so much vehicle and pedestrian traffic heading south that they were using both causeway lanes for hours. Kincaid got out of his lorry and walked forward and was told by a sentry they were going to open one lane going north at 7 pm, which meant they had to wait another 45 minutes. "Damn," he muttered under his breath getting back into the lorry, "we'll never get on with this mission." Finally the lorry in front of Kincaid's began to move. Desai shifted the Bedford into gear and they lurched forward. Approaching the bridge the military police brought them to another halt when a Sergeant in full battle dress walked over to Lt. Kincaid's side of the lorry.

"Sir, may I see your orders?" asked the Sergeant.

Kincaid produced the single page order and when the sergeant read the last line he snapped to attention, handed the orders back to Kincaid, saluted and said "proceed." He returned the salute and pointed forward to Beng who roared across the causeway followed by the lorry carrying Sergeant Standish.

As they entered the city of Johore Bahru they could see the extensive bomb damage and smoking ruins left and right and the familiar sight of refuges everywhere. They continued north through the city. Kincaid told corporal Beng to look for the Kota Tinggi trail sign and he responded he knew exactly where it was. After another 30 minutes or so they were at the turn. It was now dark when he told Beng to pull over to the side of the road, where they stopped. The second lorry came to a stop behind them and Sergeant Standish jumped out of his lorry and ran up to Lt. Kincaid who was now outside and lighting up another smoke.

"Care for a smoke Sergeant?" Kincaid asked holding a pack out to Standish.

"Don't mind if I do Lieutenant," Standish replied as he pulled a smoke from the pack which Kincaid lit for him.

"You know sergeant," Kincaid continued, "today has been a crazy day for me. It began by me following orders to get some artillery shells and mortar rounds to take back to Tebong Station and then the next thing I know I'm having a smoke seated in front of General Percivel at command headquarters, and now I'm having a smoke with you on the road to Kota Tinggi. Tomorrow at this time we'll all be back where we're supposed to be, I hope. Now Corporal Beng says the road ahead is bad and will take maybe three hours to go the 15 kilometers to our destination. We're not going to stop, so tell the men this is the last time to stretch their legs and attend any personal business."

Standish acknowledged his understanding with a nod, stamped out his cigarette and walked to the back of each lorry telling the men to get out and stretch their legs, which they all did. Soon everyone climbed back into their lorries and the journey to Taman Sri shrine began with the four sacks of gold only Kincaid knew about. He opened the map and by torchlight shining on it felt confident he could find the shrine and get back to fortress Singapore fast. Slowly they drove north east on the bumpy road when the rain started. Again Kincaid muttered "damn" under is breath as Beng switched on the wipers to clear the windshield. Corporal Beng had his hands glued to the wheel and kept the speed as fast as the roadway, which was turning into a muddy trail could bear. After an hour the rain stopped making the go a little easier. Soon they started passing staff cars and lorries of the 22nd Australian Brigade loaded with men and dragging artillery pieces heading to Singapore. He turned to Beng and commented on the procession they were passing. To the left and right he could see houses and huts and was sure the local inhabitants were nervously watching this parade from the dark shadows. Just then a head popped into the cab from the back.

"Lt. Sir," Private Alsip said, "can you tell us what's in those sacks? Kind of feels like they're full of coins."

"Wish I knew Private," Kincaid responded, "they never told me, but I can say this, whatever is inside is important enough for the Army to send us all out here to the middle of nowhere."

Kincaid knew he lied to Alsip, but that was all he could say. Revealing more would only cause more problems. Finally, two hours later, Beng pointed out a road marker to the side of the road with the words 'Taman Sri 5 km' painted in faint lettering.

"Great news," Kincaid said to Beng, "we're getting real close to the turn off, which should be on our right, just ahead."

After a few more kilometers a side road appeared that could only be the turn off to the old shrine. No other roads were marked on the map so this had to be it. Kincaid told Corporal Beng to turn up the side road. This was truly a trail and they barely made it through with the jungle foliage brushing both sides of the lorry as they proceeded several kilometers. A winding turn to the left and the small shrine appeared in the headlights. It was now close to 11 pm when he told Beng to stop near the shrine. The other lorry pulled up beside theirs and the motors were turned off. Sergeant Standish came over to Lt. Kincaid who got out of his lorry torch in hand.

"Sergeant," he said, "we made it safe and sound, now I want you and the men to scout a good place to bury these sacks, so no one will ever know we've been here. Let's step lively and get this done."

Standish repeated the order to the men and they all scattered with their torches to find a suitable burial plot and that was exactly what they found. Next to the shrine was a small abandoned cemetery. It was decided that they could easily cut the sod, bury the sacks and replace the sod so no one would know, and that is what Kincaid ordered. As the men were carefully cutting the sod and excavating the ground near one grave for the burial, Kincaid was busy looking at the map coordinates and where the road and shrine were featured, which was not exactly as presented. He took his pencil and wrote down on the map the exact map coordinates of the gold burial site, which were latitude 1 degree 44 minutes west, and longitude 103 degrees 55 minutes north. He then pulled out his Zippo lighter, pulled it apart and with his pocket knife, carefully scratched the coordinates on the inner housing by torchlight. He also scratched the word 'grave' at the bottom. He reassembled his lighter and did what Percivel had ordered him to do; he burned his orders and the map. As the flames flickered out, he placed his Zippo lighter back in his breast pocket with his cigarettes.

In another 30 minutes, the men had completed the 'sack' burial and were standing back at the lorries talking softly and clearly anxious to get out of there. Kincaid accompanied Sergeant Standish to inspect the burial site and both agreed, no one would ever know that that ground had been disturbed. They walked swiftly back to the lorries and waiting men.

"Men," Kincaid said, "a great job, now let's get the hell out of here and back to Singapore.

"Here, here," came the collective voices of the men .

"Refuel both lorries and we're off," Kincaid said. "On the way, I want you to toss out the empty flimsies and the shovels one by one. In three and one half hours we'll be back across the causeway."

Chapter **5**

In another ten minutes the lorries were fueled and headed out of the shrine trail and in another ten minutes turned and were heading southwest on the Kota Tinggi road back to Singapore. There were no other trucks on the road. Everyone was very relaxed and relieved the mission was over. Ten minutes drive time later, Private Alsip in one lorry and Perth in the other began tossing out the empty flimsies one by one and next the extra shovels were tossed high into the bush next to the road as they sailed along. Kincaid kept his eye on the road as Corporal Beng drove a little faster because of the lightened load. Getting back to Singapore was going to be a breeze, Kincaid concluded to himself, when ahead in the distance he noticed a tree down across the road. That was odd as the road was clear at this point only hours ago. Beng took his foot off the gas pedal and the lorry slowed. Corporal Desai slowed the second lorry and Sergeant Standish put his head out the window and saw the tree across the road ahead. Instantly, he bristled and turned around and told Perth to get ready for action. Both pulled their helmets on and cocked and loaded their Sten guns. Desai also put his helmet on.

"Cut the lights and motor off," Standish told Desai, which he did while slowly stepping on the brakes.

Kincaid was still rolling forward in his lorry with headlights on when machine gun fire started to rake his vehicle from both sides of the road. Pop-pop-pop-pop-pop came the staccatos from the two 7.7mm Japanese type 99 light machine guns. The sound repeated several times. He felt a sharp pain in his left side and knew he'd been wounded and then he fell forward hitting his head on the dash and winced in pain. He could hear moaning from the back of the lorry, and from driver Beng next to him, but could do nothing about it. The lorry continued slowly on, ran into the felled palm tree across the road and stopped.

By this time Sergeant Standish was out of his lorry with Private Perth running forward while returning fire to both sides of the road with their Sten guns until their ammo was gone. While reloading with fresh clips the sound of rifle fire from behind surprised them and they were instantly cut down in a hail of bullets. Corporal Desai suffered the same fate when he tried to get out of the lorry to return fire. Now everything was quiet, except for Alsip and McKnight who were both moaning for help from inside the first lorry. Both had been severely wounded, but alive, as was Kincaid.

Lieutenant Ichido Yomeida of the Japanese 25th Army, 5th division approached the two lorries from behind walking slowly down the road, his sword dragging as he walked. A veteran of the Manchurian campaign, he welcomed the task of freeing Malaya from British colonial rule and enjoyed out flanking his adversary. Now he had captured two trucks. His men had already pulled everyone out of the vehicles and put them all on the right side of the road, dead and alive. Kincaid was coming back to consciousness and tried to stand holding his side, but his severe wound made that impossible. He remained stooped on one knee clutching his side. Yomeida shouted an order in Japanese to put flashlights on the enemy, which his troops did. He very casually told his men "no prisoners" and with that he walked up to the stooped Lt. Kincaid and shot him in the head with his revolver. As Kincaid fell forward and hit the roadway face down, the Zippo lighter came out of his breast pocket and fell before the feet of Lt. Yomeida who reached down and picked it up. As he was examining it and lighting it over and over, gunfire broke the nights quiet again as the Japanese soldiers shot Alsip and McKnight to death. Then it was quiet again, except for the echoing sound of the Zippo lighters cover snapping open and shut.

PART TWO

Chapter **6** – Singapore, Approaching Changi Airfield,

Friday, February 23, 1952, 4 pm

Another routine landing coming up after another routine round trip to Hong Kong, but this was a special day for Captain John "Cat" McCoy's copilot friend, Larson Durant, a real first class Englishmen, who was on his last cargo flight before retiring.

"Larson," Cat said looking over to his co-pilot, "You want to bring her in?"

"Absolutely," he replied with a smile, "Now gear down my boy and let papa take over."

They were laughing their way through the final landing checklist. Their plane, a Curtis C-46 Commando, named the '*Lucky Seven*' was all lined up to land when Larson switched the radio to the tower frequency.

"Changi tower, this is MalSing 7 on final 27," Larson announced in a jovial tone in his deep British accent.

"Roger MalSing 7," the tower controller replied, "proceed clear on 27."

Larson asked Cat for flaps 20 as he basked in the sun streaming into the cockpit one last time on this beautiful Friday afternoon. He looked out the window at the Straits of Johore causeway and said goodbye to this faithful navigational landing aid. He adjusted the propeller pitch controls to bite less air and tapped the throttle forward a bit as they continued on their descent. Soon the end of the runway was in sight and the *Lucky Seven'* was all trimmed and ready to land. He pulled back the throttles and floated in to a two point landing and then dropped the tail ever so carefully without a bounce.

"Well done Papa," Cat said, "I'm going to miss your perfect landings my friend."

They taxied across the field to the MalSing Air Charter Service hanger, which was on the opposite side of this military airfield and brought the plane to a stop. Larson switched off the magnetos and the two powerful Pratt and Whitney radial engines slowly went quiet.

"I can't believe we've been together two years," Cat said, "it seems only yesterday we started this flying adventure with Larry Chen."

"I know. Time flies when you're having fun old boy," Larson replied, "but all things come to an end and its time for me to kick back a little."

Cat flew C-46's over the 'hump' from India to Kunming, China with the US 7th Air Force during the last few months of World War II. After mustering out of the Army he eventually returned to Shanghai, China to fly for Claire Chennault in his newly created China Air Transport airline. This was before the communists took over the mainland. In 1948 the airline moved to Taiwan. He considered Chennault to be one of the finest

31

pilots and leaders he had ever known. He continued flying air cargo from Taiwan to all of Southeast Asia until 1950, when a well to do and well connected Chinese business friend, Larry Chen, hired him away to help start up an air cargo service out of the British Crown Colony of Singapore. Larry had purchased five war surplus planes in the United States, two DC-3's and three C-46's to start his freight charter service. Then age 32, Cat thought this was going to be exciting and an adventure in itself, so he joined on. He loved to fly and thanks to the US Army fell in love with India, China and all Southeast Asia. These were exotic places he had only read about at home in Evanston, Illinois before the war, but something deep inside him wanted to continue doing what he loved, flying in exotic places and the money was fantastic, more than twice what he could earn at home.

However, from the exciting part at the beginning, routine became somewhat of the norm in the last year and that wasn't all that bad, and maybe he was finally growing up, but that was no fun!

He knew the C-46 Commando like the back of his hand. It was a powerful work horse, quirky, but solid and in all his post war years, the C-46 always got him safely to the ground, which is not to say he didn't pucker up a few times and have those moments of total terror pilots have once in a blue moon to include close calls, near misses, mechanical breakdowns, bad gas, no brakes, but all in all life was good. Now it was time to celebrate the retirement of his friend and colleague Larson.

Larson my friend, it's been a pleasure to fly with you these past two years. I hope retirement suits you." Cat said with a big smile.

"Likewise my friend, we'll meet again in the future, someplace, some time I hope," he replied.

They shook hands, unbuckled and got up from their cockpit seats together for the last time.

"I will miss this old girl more than you know," Larson said, "She's been a wonderful part of my life."

Both men walked back through the cargo bay past the crates and boxes netted to the cargo floor on their way to the exit door, which was now opened by the third member of the crew, Lling Munai, a Malaysian who was their cargo master, flight mechanic, radio man and chief cook and bottle washer. He cared for the 'Lucky Seven' like no other crew man Cat had worked with. They climbed down the ladder one at a time with Larson stopping and taking one last look at the inside of the Lucky Seven. He was a little apprehensive and embarrassed about tonight's send off party for him at the Raffles Hotel, but resigned himself that it would be fun, as Cat had planned this great send off for months.

Upon setting foot on the tarmac, they were unexpectedly greeted by the owner, Larry Chen, who after shaking hands with Cat and Larson, asked Cat to speak with him privately. Cat patted Larson on the back and said he would be right along and for him to take the paperwork to the office.

"What's up Boss," Cat said.

"Tomorrow morning be in office at 9 am for meeting with executive manager from the Malaysia Oil Exploration Company. We've been asked to assist with an emergency rescue mission. Seems one of their senior scientists had a serious accident and broke both his legs in a remote part of Malaysia. We are their only hope to get him out safely and to hospital. They want us to retrieve him and then fly him to Hong Kong for treatment." Larry said.

"Hey, no problem boss can do," he said, "but why can't they get him out overland?"

33

"To serious a break is what they told me. They've dropped in a Doctor to stabilize him until we can pluck him out," Larry replied.

"What do you mean pluck him out?" Cat asked quizzically.

"Just be in my office tomorrow morning and you'll get your answers. They have already paid for the trip in advance, at triple the weekly rate, plus fuel. I couldn't say no to that dough," Larry chuckled.

With that Cat nodded and smiled and the two men walked to the hanger office where he met up with Larson talking with Jasmine Chen, who Cat was strongly attracted. Well more than strongly attracted. How about strongly in love with Jasmine, but from afar. She was the boss's beautiful raven haired daughter and worked in the office with her father and her uncle. She also had the same strong feelings for Cat well hidden inside. She was very smart and well educated, having finished her education in London and spoke excellent English. Her eyes lit up when Cat came into the office with her father. She was very cool on the surface about this and doubly good about keeping her feelings under wraps; however, it was becoming clear that they both wanted to be together, but how to make this work given all the local taboos. After giving each other 'the look' and exchanging their usual office talk for all to hear, Cat knew this was going to be difficult and now was not the time or place to take things any further. Larson was finishing up going over the flight paperwork and cargo manifest with Jasmine.

"Ready for some refreshment Larson?" Cat quipped stepping beside Larson across the counter from Jasmine while looking only her face.

"Does a frog need water?" Larson replied.

"And you, Jasmine, are you coming to the party?" Cat casually allowed to roll off his tongue, hoping that she would say yes.

"Of course I'll be there," Jasmine replied, "It will be an honor to say goodbye to Mr. Durant," she said smiling with a glance to both of them.

Cat's heart began racing a bit at that good news, and hoped he would have a few moments alone with his secret 'pipperoo'. He had so much to say to her and never the right opportunity.

"Larson, let's get you to Raffles pronto," Cat said as they started to walk out to the parking area and then got into Cat's old Land Rover. He reached in the back and pulled out two Cuban Churchill cigars from a box and handed one to Larson. They fired them up and headed toward downtown Singapore puffing on those delightful smokes, talking back and forth and laughing.

"It just doesn't get any better than this," Cat blared out as he concentrated on keeping the Land Rover on the left side of the road, which he never really got used to. As they slowly drove the two lane road, they bantered back and forth about people they had encountered and all the highlights and unusual events and circumstances they had gone through these past two years.

Chapter 7

Arriving at Raffles Hotel on Beach Road, Cat parked outside and both men strode to the entrance of the famous hotel and into the long bar.

"Run a tab Jonny," Cat said to his favorite bartender as he sauntered in, "We're celebrating the retirement of one of the finest pilots on the planet."

Already in the bar were three of the other MalSing flight crews. Larson enjoyed numerous handshakes, greetings, pats on the back. As the bar continued to fill with pilots and friends of Larson, including many British RAF pilots from the Changi base, soon all were hoisting their glasses time and again in his honor. Toasts were coming one after another. The piano player was fingering the lively Glenn Miller tune 'In the Mood' and continued on playing everyone's favorites. The drinks kept coming and coming and coming.

Larry Chen arrived within the hour with Jasmine, who had changed into a stunning black outfit. When they entered the bar and everyone noticed her merchandise the din got toned down a bit, but not by much. Cat was staring at her in awe as she walked in. Larry walked over to the piano player and asked him to stop for a moment, as Jasmine followed behind with all eyes on her. When the music stopped, a hush came over the bar and all faced a smiling Larry.

"Larson, come over here," he said waiving and speaking in his best English.

Larson stepped next to Larry Chen and Jasmine and turned back towards the throng hugging the long bar.

"Larson, in appreciation for long good service to the Company, we give you this watch," he said with a huge smile on his face. The watch was handed to Larson, who blushed and tried to remain calmer than he normally does, but the booze had him totally charged up in a relaxed strictly British way.

"I want to thank you Mr. Chen for the watch," he said as he accepted the engraved watch, shook his hand and then held up the watch for all to see as applause filled the long bar from all gathered.

"I will miss all you wonderful people," he said with a tearful smile. Another round of applause filled the room with lots of 'here here's.'

"Three cheers for Larson," someone shouted out, and everyone toned in with "hip hip hooray, hip hip hooray, hip hip hooray."

Jasmine stepped next to Larson and gave him a big kiss on the cheek leaving a ruby red lip kiss behind, which brought more loud applause, whistles and razing from the gathered throng. Larson was in seventh heaven. The piano player began playing 'For he's a jolly good fellow,' and everyone joined in singing. Soon the song ended with more applause and it was like a switch was turned on again and the bar rocked.

Soon another Glenn Miller hit, the Chattanooga Choo Choo was being played to a lively tempo. All were enjoying the camaraderie of the moment. A huge Chinese buffet dim sum dinner was then rolled in the bar on several serving carts and the assembled hoard wasted no time in helping themselves to the scrumptious food.

Jasmine walked over to Cat who was standing at the bar observing the goings on and stood close.

"Can you give a girl a light," she asked Cat extending a cigarette retrieved from her purse in her best Lauren Bacall low sultry voice. Cat was speechless. He grabbed a pack of matches on the bar, fumbled in tearing out a single match and eventually got it to light on the third try. Jasmine reached out with her right hand and held his hand steady holding the match and ever so slowly pulled it toward the cigarette she held to her mouth. When Cat saw it was lit he pulled his hand away, but Jasmine pulled his back closer to her face and gently blew the match out while never taking her eyes off him. Only then did she let his hand go. Cat remained speechless and continued to look lovingly in stunned amazement at her face. Transfixed was the proper word to describe this encounter between them.

"Jasmine," Cat said over the noise of the party, "I've so much to talk to you about, but never have found the right time, or place or way. I don't think your family would approve."

Jasmine took a small puff on her cigarette and looked at him with a blushed faint smile.

"Cat, our time is coming," she said in her sultry voice with eyes aglow that soon spread into a perfect smile for him alone.

Before Cat could say anything further, Larry Chen walked up to the both of them.

"Jasmine, we must be going. I can't leave you here with all these tigers and besides, it late and we full day tomorrow," he said smiling at both of them, not letting on he knew they were in love with each other. "And Cat, see you tomorrow morning, nine am sharp for sure?"

Cat nodded. They all exchanged their goodbyes and then Jasmine winked at Cat as they both turned and walked out of the bar. Cat watched Jasmine's lovely outline every second until she was gone and knew he had to talk with Larry about the very delicate matter of his daughter and his feelings for her real soon. While his mind was totally absorbed with Jasmine, Larson came up from behind and tapped him on the shoulder.

"Say mate, what say we grab a couple of drinks and head outside for some fresh air," he happily said being almost three sheets to the wind.

"You got it my friend. Drambuie on the rocks work for you?" he said grinning.

"Roger that," Larson said a bit tipsily.

After Cat had the drinks in hand they headed out the side door to the patio garden area near the pool, found two comfortable chairs and sat down. Cat passed the drink to Larson, who sipped the sweet orangey flavored nectar and put the glass down on the table. Two more Cuban robusto cigars appeared from Cat's flying jacket and both men lit up for the last time. It was after ten pm and the piano music from the bar had toned down a bit to softer melodies that drifted their way. Cat reflected how there's something wonderful about piano music that can add clarity to any moment. Drinks in hand, Cat toasted his colleague and wished him well and God speed, as their glasses clinked one last time.

"Now Larson, be sure to write and tell us what your retirement is like," Cat said knowing full well that would probably never happen, however the sentiment was still there.

"I'll write you every week…Promise." Larson replied puffing on his cigar.

The cigar smoke swirled and rose in the still night air as the two friends finished their nightcaps and their cigars. Soon thereafter they returned to the bar. Larson paid his farewells to all those gathered, waved goodbye and slowly walked out of the Long Bar, through the Raffles lobby and out to Cat's Land Rover. Cat was waiting in the driveway when Larson hopped in his seat.

"Home James," Larson said to Cat pointing north.

Cat started up his Land Rover, dropped her grindingly into first gear and they lurched out of the hotel parking lot and headed north to the Changi airport area with a first stop at Larson's apartment. After another merry drive singing 'Waltzing Matilda" together they arrived at Larson's place and Cat turned off the motor.

"Goodbye Larson," Cat said as he shook his hand again and bid him fond farewell.

"Take care Cat ole boy and be good to *Lucky Seven*," Larson said in a somewhat somber and melancholy tone with words ever so slightly slurred to perfection.

Larson got out of the Land Rover, reached back in to shake Cat's hand and slowly turned and walked up the steps to his apartment building. Cat started his Land Rover and slowly drove off up the road two kilometers to his top floor apartment near the airfield at 963 Upper Changi Road. He parked and switched off the motor and walked up the three flights of stairs to apartment 3C. Turning the key in the lock signaled to his tired brain he was glad to finally be home.

As he stepped into his apartment and switched on the dim overhead entry light he could smell the faint hint of lingering perfume on his first breath. Looking across the dark apartment he could see someone standing in the balcony door looking back. It was Jasmine. Cat froze, not knowing what to say or do and continued to look at Jasmine while half in and half out the door. Finally he stepped in and pushed the door closed behind him as Jasmine rushed up to kiss him without saying a word. The first kiss of new love. She pushed him back against the door. His mind was spinning again as the object of his affection seemed to have the same idea he had been thinking about, but afraid to act upon. Cat held her tightly as they continued to embrace. The moment he had planned, but was unprepared for was here. He was intoxicated by her. Soon the long kiss stopped. The embrace slowly ended and she stepped back looking him in the eyes. They were now holding each others hands.

"Welcome home Cat," Jasmine said, with her wonderfully coy smile, dark eyes and sultry voice he had grown to love from afar. The forbidden fruit was before him, his emotions were now running at 110%. The woman he secretly loved from afar was now so near. Did she have the same feelings for him? Obviously yes was the answer!

"Jasmine, what are you doing here," Cat replied stupidly as his brain was working hard on what to do and say next. For the first time in his life he was slightly befuddled with the situation.

"No wait, Jasmine, I know why you are here," Cat blurted out while continuing to look at her face, "It's just there's trouble in all this, if we go too far. Your father, won't approve. I know what the rules are around here."

"We'll deal with that later," she replied walking backward and pulling him by both arms into the apartment and up to the rattan sofa.

"Tell me one thing," she said softly, looking him in the eyes, "Do you love me?"

"Yes", Cat replied as he fell next to her in an embrace on the sofa. His hand slowly stroked the side of her face and her hair as his soul breathed in her essence. They soon were intertwined in love that only ended with the morning sun streaming in the window.

"Now what?" Cat thought to himself as he looked lovingly at the sleeping beauty next to him. Had Cat found his kitty? Obviously!

Chapter **8**

The early February Singapore Saturday morning was comfortably temperate as Cat turned the key in the Land Rover for the short drive to the MalSing Air Charter Services offices at Changi field. He was dressed in a fresh khaki uniform, but hadn't put his tie on yet. He left Jasmine behind, still sleeping. There was so much more he wanted to say to her that he almost considered bagging the meeting with Larry Chen and returning upstairs to his apartment. However, duty called, even if he was dead tired and slightly hung-over. The smile on his face just thinking about Jasmine made him feel better, however the one hour nap he had wouldn't do and he knew it.

"Tough it out ole boy," he said to himself.

Cat drove slowly around the side of the hanger, parked and slowly walked into the empty pilot's ready room which adjoined the offices' just before 8 am. His goal: an hour to wakeup, sober up, clear his head, and be ready for his 9 am meeting.

He seemed to be feeling that all too familiar hangover haze that only strong coffee would cure. Meandering to the break area kitchen, he grabbed the percolator, filled it with water and heaped 5 scopes of coffee into the basket and pushed the 'on' switch. The two aspirin he took in the apartment were also starting to do their job and the dull throbbing in his head was slowly going away. Soon the smell of fresh coffee aroma filled the air as the percolator made its normal burbling sound. He sat down on a nearby chair and with eyes closed held his head for a few minutes with both hands, elbows firmly planted on his knees. When the percolator stopped, he got up and poured a mug of that hot restorative brew, laced it with just the right amount of canned milk and sugar and sat back down sipping the nectar that would finally shake away the mythical god Morpheus's grip on him…for a while anyway.

As the aspirin and coffee did their job, Cat's senses slowly came back to normal. He couldn't stop thinking about Jasmine and couldn't stop from smiling at the same time. Why did he say he'd do this silly rescue mission, whatever it was, and ruin his one day off. Something just didn't add up. Where were they going to land to get the injured geologist on board? This sounds like they need one of those new helicopters to save this man. The questions were forming faster and faster in his head as he continued to sip, then gulp his first cup of coffee down.

Soon a second cup of joe was in his hand and he walked into the washroom to straighten up for the meeting. He put on his tie, while looking at himself in the mirror. That grin would not go away. There was a glow inside him that he had never felt before in all his 35 years. It was the inner glow known only to lovers. Hair combed and presentable, he downed the second cup of coffee and walked back into the ready room. A truck appeared outside and headed toward the parked *Lucky Seven* sitting on the tarmac. Another car followed the truck. As he wondered what was going on, Larry Chen walked into the room and beckoned for Cat to follow him. It was a quarter to 9 as he walked into the deserted main office, following Larry into his office. The man seated in front of Larry's desk stood up and faced Cat as he entered.

"Cat, I want you meet Mr. Jefferies, General Manager Malaysian Oil Exploration," Larry said. Cat extended his hand and both men shook hands, smiling politely to each other.

"Mr. Chen has told me a lot about you Captain McCoy," Jeffries said as he looked Cat in the eyes. "He says you're the best transport pilot in Singapore."

"Thank you Mr. Jeffries," Cat replied in a friendly tone. "I paid him to say that, you know," as everyone chuckled over these pleasantries.

"Please, please sit down," Larry intoned motioning for both men to sit down in the chairs before his desk. "Cat, Mr. Jeffries is the gentleman that chartered the 'Lucky Seven' to rescue his injured chief geologist and fly him to Hong Kong. He has two severely broken legs."

"Why don't you just transport him by bearers to the nearest road and drive him out to the nearest airport," Cat said looking directly at Jeffries.

"Wish we could," Jeffries replied. "The doctor we parachuted in radioed last night the leg breaks are too severe and he is in excruciating pain. Total immobilization is the only answer. Minimal movement is necessary, yes mandated in this case to save his life. We'll extract him from our remote Malaysian base camp tomorrow morning and fly him immediately to Hong Kong for treatment."

"If you parachuted a doctor in, where is it I am to land exactly?" Cat said quizzically.

Jeffries quickly turned and looked straight at Larry Chen. "You mean you didn't tell him how we were going to do this extraction?" Jeffries said rather miffed.

"Sorry. No chance yesterday. Why don't you explain," Larry replied.

"Captain McCoy, you are not landing," Jeffries uttered directly to Cat. "We'll employ the Brazilian mail service technique for the extraction using a stretcher basket which you'll winch onboard your C-46. The entire rescue will only take 20 to 30 minutes to get our Geologist and the Doctor on board and we're off to Hong Kong, Kai Tac airport."

Cat sat forward, floored at what he was hearing and looked at both Jeffries and Larry Chen in a dumbfounded manner and asked, "Now exactly what about this Brazilian mail service technique?"

"Oh, you've not heard of it before?" Jeffries asked.

"No," Cat replied in a skeptical mode. "Enlighten me please."

Jeffries leaned forward and opened his brief case and pulled out a *Popular Mechanics* magazine, opened it to an article and handed it to Cat.

"This should fully explain the technique, which is used to lower and retrieve mail in the land locked Amazon jungles of Brazil," Jefferies said as he reached over and handed the magazine to Cat as he pointed to the photograph of a DC-3 aircraft performing the maneuver. "You'll fly in a 30 degree banked circle around the target at 500 to 750 feet while the basket is lowered. It stays centered in the circle. Then when our patient is strapped in, the high speed winch will haul him in. Piece of cake for you ole boy," Jeffries concluded.

"I don't know about this," Cat exclaimed, leaning back in his chair while stretching out his legs.

"Well, Mr. Chen here says you could do this maneuver in your sleep. You are the best pilot in Singapore aren't you? Jeffries questioned.

Larry Chen piped up. "Cat, you can do this in your sleep. No problem. Just fly in circle. Piece of cake for you," he said smiling to Cat and Jeffries. "And Mr. Jeffries's men installing winch equipment now. When done and you comfortable with everything, take off this afternoon at one pm for practice run up near Taman Sri. Build some confidence. Piece of cake? Yes?" he said.

Cat was still leaning back in his chair looking at the magazine article in disbelief while sorting this out in his mind. He knew the deck was stacked against him. Larry needed the easy money in this deal, but there were unforeseen risks here. What if we have an accident? What if the patient dies? He thought to himself. After a long silence he had no other choice, but to say yes. Slowly he sat up in his chair and put the magazine down on his lap. All eyes were focused on Cat's tired, sullen, expressionless face and eyes. Then he mustered up a huge smile for Larry and Jeffries and said, "No problem. Piece of cake."

"Fine," Larry Chen said smiling, "Mr. Jeffries will be traveling with you on practice run and will assist with the extraction test. He has a man to operate the winch equipment, so Lling Munai won't have to worry about that. All will be ready before noon."

"Excellent then," Jeffries replied as he stood up and shook Larry's hand and then Cat's. "I'm going out to the plane to see how the winch installation is progressing." And with that he left the office.

Cat sat back down again, magazine in hand and stared quizzically at Larry Chen. He asked him if the triple pay to charter the *Lucky Seven'* was really worth it. He knew the answer before Larry responded.

"Cat," he said, "You can do this and yes, we need the money and I have the money already in the bank. They paid in cash yesterday and its more than triple rate. They paid for the equivalent of two weeks of flying plus fuel. This job will only take you two days at most. You'll be right back and can take a few days off. And there's a big bonus for you upon completion. Everyone wins on this deal."

"And Boss, with Larson gone I need a new co-pilot," Cat casually tossed out very nonchalantly.

"No problem Cat," Larry replied, "your new co-pilot is already here, checked out, licensed and assisting with the winch installation as we speak. Let's go out to the plane to meet co-pilot," Larry said.

"Ok Boss," Cat replied as both men got up and walked out of the office, through the hanger and onto the tarmac where the *Lucky Seven'* was buzzing like a bee with activity in the mid morning sun.

Chapter **9**

As Cat and Larry Chen walked slowly toward the *'Lucky Seven'* , he could see the truck with Malaysian Oil Exploration Ltd painted on the door backed up to the plane's cargo door. As they approached, Cat could see the winch apparatus poking out the cargo door. Cat reached the cargo door ladder first and began to climb up. As he reached the top a hand was thrust out from inside which he instantly gripped pulling himself up into the cargo bay. As he looked up the arm his eyes were greeted by a very attractive, smiling woman with dirty blondish hair partially stuffed under a baseball cap. She was wearing mechanic overalls complete with high top combat boots. Cat immediately noticed she completely filled out her overalls.

"Hello," she said in a very proper, but sultry British voice,

"I'm Trish Mathews, your new copilot."

Cat's mouth dropped open as he released her hand and stood straight up in the cargo bay. Nothing immediately came out of his mouth, as the second surprise within one hour was standing and smiling at him. It was almost more than he could take. Before Cat could say anything she continued.

"Mr. Chen has told me so much about you and I'm honored to be your second in command. I've only flown a C-46 once on a ferry mission, but am fully checked out, type rated and ready to go. I have read the operating manual again from cover to cover and just completed the ground school classes and passed the certification test with flying colors. I've over 1500 hours in the Dakota, flying in Canada, England and the outback in Australia," Trish said.

Cat continued to stand there looking at Trish, saying nothing as Larry Chen came up the ladder and stepped into the cargo bay.

"Ah, I see you two have met," Larry said with a grin on his face as he reached out and shook Trish's hand. Turning to Cat he continued, "She has excellent credentials. Was RAF ferry pilot in World War II. You'll have many war stories to tell each other," Larry said chuckling looking back and forth at both of them with a smile.

Cat bit his lip really hard to stay composed and figured now was not the time to discuss this new situation with Larry in front of his new 'blonde bombshell' co-pilot.

"Well hello Miss Mathews," Cat said politely mustering all the self control he could find inside, "and how is the winch installation going?

Trish pulled what appeared to be installation plans from her pocket and replied.

"I've studied these in detail and everything is proceeding as indicated and on schedule," she said in a very business like manner. She pointed to the one mechanic tightening the floor bolts on the winch frame and to another mechanic who was installing electrical cables to a control panel installed on the bulkhead by the door. Another mechanic was just finishing securing to the cargo bay floor a large metal box. Trish said it contained the batteries necessary to power the winch. She also pointed out that electrical service was already connected to the C-46's system to run the battery charger bolted next to the battery box. Cat looked closely at the entire set-up and could immediately tell this was high quality custom equipment designed specifically for this rescue. He looked at Trish.

"Miss Mathews, do you think this contraption will work? Cat asked.

"Well Captain McCoy," Trish responded, "from what I've read in the specifications, the winch equipment will definitely lift an injured man of 250 pounds or more in that metal basket," she said pointing to the basket leaning against the opposite bulkhead. "This winch has a high speed DC motor that will lift 10 ft per second in high gear. This should bring the basket up 1000 feet in under two minutes, but I'd run it a lot slower than that to be safe."

Cat knew that Larry must have briefed her fully on this rescue mission, knowing he would not say no. At least she was comfortable with the device, but why did he not feel good about all this. He wondered why everyone knew what he was going to do, or was Larry just playing the odds, after all, he had other pilots to take this mission if he decided not to do it. Larry also knew the other guys would jump at the extra pay. Just then one of the mechanics motioned to Trish. She excused herself and walked forward in the cargo bay and started talking with the mechanic. Cat asked Larry to step off the plane to talk. Both men climbed down the ladder onto the tarmac. Stepping away from the doorway Cat was ready to pounce on Larry and give him a tongue lashing, but again he restrained himself.

"Larry, I thought you were going to assign Tom Boland as my co-pilot. Where did she come from?" he asked gesturing back at the plane.

"Oh, Aussie Outback Air. They owed me big favor and we need another pilot pronto. You teach her good. She all business. No problem Cat. Jasmine even say OK." He replied.

Why had he brought Jasmine into this he wondered? All this was just too hard to believe, or was this another of Larry's tests of character. Did he somehow know of Jasmine's feelings for me?

"OK Larry," I'll train her and break her in, but if she can't handle any of this, she's gone," Cat exclaimed.

"Fair enough," Larry replied. "Got to go. See you later at take off." Then he turned and walked back into the office.

Cat climbed back up into the cargo bay of the *Lucky Seven*' and began looking at the winch apparatus, cables and controls close up. He could see the mechanics were almost done with the installation. Trish walked up next to Cat as he was inspecting the control box.

"Captain, I've been briefed on how all this equipment works, but we don't have to operate it as their mechanic will ride with us to operate it.

"Did Larry Chen explain the flying maneuver necessary to make this work?" Cat asked.

"Yes", she replied, "I've heard of this banked 30 degree circle flying maneuver before, but don't know anyone who has ever done it, however, it seems pretty straight forward. My concern was about snagging something, but they have two breakaway links equally spaced in the cable that will snap at a 750 pound tug, so this risk appears minimal. We even have a spare basket and extra cable if that happens. Thank God we're doing this in full daylight and from what I understand from Mr. Jefferies, the pickup location will be a cleared circle of 250 feet diameter or more. I think we can do this and save that poor man's life."

"At least we'll have practice this afternoon to test all this equipment," he said

"Sounds good to me," Trish responded as Cat looked at her very attractive face and decided two things right then. First he would attempt this rescue and second, he decided to give her the benefit of the doubt. She seemed knowledgeable and competent, and apart from being a woman, and beautiful at that, was impressed by her take charge attitude in learning the winch apparatus. Looking over her shoulder he noticed the mechanics installing two parachute harnesses on a long tether buckled opposite the door. Trish turned to see what Cat was looking at.

"Oh, those are for the winch operator and Mr. Jeffries to pull in the basket so they won't fall out at that 30 degree angle," she said, "Seems they have thought of everything."

"Miss Mathews," Cat said, "please finish observing the winch install and find Lling Munai, my flight engineer and have the 'Lucky Seven' fueled and ready for our one o'clock take off. "

"Eye, eye Cap," she said with a smile on her face as she saluted in the British manner stamping her boots at attention.

Chapter **10**

Cat turned and climbed down the ladder and went back into the pilot's ready room. Down deep inside he thought the whole idea was crazy to attempt such a rescue mission. Something just didn't add up in all this. If that geologist was injured just yesterday, how could they have gotten this winch apparatus assembled on such short notice? All this hardware to save just one man? Anyway, Cat decided to roll with the punches. Where was Larson when he really needed him most? Just one more day. Just one more day to have steady Larson on this flight. Cat grabbed his mug and poured another cup of joe and sat down with the *Popular Mechanics* article to read in detail. He had two hours to absorb all this before take off. He finished reading the article in half an hour and was going over the flight sequence in his mind when Jefferies walked in the door.

"There you are old boy," Jefferies said as he walked up to Cat carrying a map. "Wanted to show you where we're going for the practice mission and then rescue early tomorrow morning."

Jefferies spread the map out on the table and pointed first to the practice area near Taman Sri, and then to the central Malaysia mountain rescue area near Labis. Two large 'X's' had been penciled in to show the locations. Cat looked closely at it for a moment.

"Are you sure everything's been cleared back over 250 feet from the center of each pickup area?" Cat asked. "I don't want to snag anything. I'm very concerned about a mishap"

"Yes, all is cleared and they told me they were ready in the last radio broadcast," Jefferies said, "not to worry, you'll do splendid!"

"Now explain something to me Mr. Jefferies," Cat asked, "How did you assemble all this custom equipment in one day?"

"Oh that was easy," he said, "We ordered this setup months ago for installation in our DC-3 for just this type of situation. The main reason for the gear was to extract ore and drilling core samples and take them for analysis daily to our lab in Kuala Lumpur. The second reason was to lower sensitive, heavy and expensive electronic equipment without damage. I can assure you we would have handled this rescue ourselves, but unfortunately, our plane had an accident landing last week and is on the mend as we speak. Timing couldn't have been worse for us."

"Oh, I see," Cat said in a low tone. "And I hear from my co-pilot, Miss Mathews, that you and one of your mechanics will be operating the equipment."

"Of course," he said, "That's the deal! You get us to the pickup point and bank the plane and we'll handle the rest. Piece of cake."

"Yes," Cat replied, "Piece of cake."

"I've got a few last minute telephone calls to make. See you at take off," he said as he turned and walked into the main office. As he opened the door, Trish Mathews was heading into the pilot's office carrying a suitcase and a valise. She stopped at the table where Cat was hunched over looking at the map.

"Are those our pickup destinations?" she asked.

Cat stood up and casually replied "yes, both in the middle of nowhere."

"Captain, may I talk freely," she asked while looking around the room to be sure no one was there.

"Of course Miss Mathews," he said, "what's the problem."

"I want to apologize for this morning, my first day on the job," she said. "I'm sure I was a shock to you as I have been for just about everyone who first meets me. Don't know what I do to people, but I apologize. Can't do anything about being a woman or the package, but I do love flying and the smell of aviation gas and will do whatever it takes to prove to you I can do the job. When Larry Chen offered me the job to be your co-pilot, I was thrilled at the chance to fly C-46's throughout Asia. It's not easy being a woman in this man's game."

She opened her valise and pull out some papers.

"Here are my credentials and references, if you want to check me out," she said as she handed the papers to Cat. "I really appreciate your giving me a chance. I do have a chance, don't I?"

Cat sat down at the table and looked through her credentials and flying history, which started in England in 1944. He could see she had extensive flying experience as a ferry pilot and became fascinated that she had flown several P-51 Mustangs from Canada via Newfoundland back to England. In many respects she had more experience in more types of aircraft than he did and many of his colleagues. He finished looking at the two pages and handed them back to Trish.

"I guess you've had to be 'twice as good' as a man to be accepted 'just as good' as a man in the flying game," Cat said.

"Trish, may I call you Trish?" He asked as she nodded back. "Trish, just do your job and we'll get along fine. I am happy to train you on the C-46, a rather unforgiving plane until you master her quirks. If Larry Chen thinks you have what it takes, then so do I. He has an uncanny eye for talent, only collecting the best. So you've hooked up with a really good outfit, the ole MalSing Air Charter Service. Welcome aboard!"

He reached over the table with his hand and she grabbed it and shook it vigorously. A huge smile had formed on her face.

"Oh thank you so much," she said. "Please excuse me while I change into my flying uniform." With that she walked into the washroom. Cat just smiled shaking his head as he followed her walk.

"Oh my God," Cat muttered to himself, "what's next?"

Lling Munai walked into the pilot's room and Cat turned to see who entered.

"Captain Cat the plane is fueled and ready," he said.

"Great Lling, now can you get a weather report from the air base? He asked.

"Already done. Here is report," he said handing it to Cat.

"Outstanding, and be sure we have some sandwiches and drinks on the plane," Cat said.

"Sandwiches already on board," he said as he turned and walked out the door to the hangar again.

Trish reappeared wearing her flight khaki's and her well worn A-2 leather flight jacket, complete with RAF ferry pilot insignia and her navy blue baseball cap. Keeping her blond locks all under cover was not working.

"Oh Trish, good, please come here and let's go over the practice flight and weather report," Cat said as she walked beside him and looked at the map. "We'll take off and head north over Johore and turn east and follow the Kota Tinggi road to the practice area here," he said pointing to the map. Now tomorrow morning we'll head north, northwest to the rescue area. The funny thing is there's a very serviceable road right here and very close, within 10 miles, of where we're going," he said pointing to the map and what appeared to be a side road heading east from Labis. "They could easily have driven closer to take their injured geologist out that way. Anyway, the weatherman says we have sunny skies CAVU[1] this afternoon and tomorrow morning."

Trish looked at the map and then at Cat.

"Captain, I agree with you, something doesn't quite add up," she said, "but this will be a first for both of us to pull off."

"Please put our flight plan together and here's your reading assignment," Cat said handing her the *Popular Mechanics* magazine. "Read the article on the mail maneuver as I go chat with Mr. Chen. We'll do the pre-flight checks at 12:30. Roger?"

"Yes sir," she replied taking the magazine and sitting down at the table.

With that, Cat left the pilots room and went into the office. Seated at her desk was a smiling Jasmine. Cat immediately perked up.

"Hello flyboy," she said. "Enjoy meeting your new co-pilot?"

---

[1] Clear and visibility unlimited.

"You knew all about this didn't you, Cat said walking up to her desk. "Why didn't you tell me last night?"

Looking around to be sure no one else was in the office she said, "Careful, Daddy wanted you to be surprised! Were you?"

"You know the answer Jasmine," he said, "why even ask? I have had more surprises in the last 12 hours than I can handle, including this crazy flight to rescue this guy in a mountain valley near Labis. And my dear Jasmine, we need to talk when I get back. I mean really talk," as that wonderful glow started to reappear on his face as he looked at her.

"Cat, please be careful," she said, "Everything will work out. Daddy say's this flight is a piece of cake for you!"

"Sure, piece of cake," he said as he turned and walked toward Larry Chen's office wondering why everyone was saying this flight was going to be a piece of cake, except me. He was getting sick of those three words.

"He's not in there Cat," she said, "I think he's aboard the 'Lucky Seven' with Mr. Jefferies."

Cat stopped and turned around and looked at Jasmine once again and walked up beside her, bent over and kissed her.

"Fine," he said as he stood up and headed out into the hangar bay and headed to the 'Lucky Seven' smiling. Jasmine sat there in her own engulfing invisible glow with a wonderful smile on her face too!

Chapter **11**

Cat walked out of the hanger towards the *Lucky Seven*. It was almost 12:30 pm. A new adventure was about to begin. He wished he could take a nap, but the strong doses of coffee and adrenaline had him wide awake and ready. Many a time he had flown exhausted over the 'hump' in India, with a lot more at risk. As he approached he could see Larry Chen and Jefferies shaking hands. Cat approached and the men turned toward him.

"Captain McCoy," Jefferies said, "our winch apparatus is installed and working perfectly. My man and I will work the winch over the pickup area. We'll make just two test pickups with twice the weight we'll have tomorrow. I think around 500 pounds per lift. Should take less than an hour for you and me to get the hang of this equipment and your flying maneuver." Tomorrow we'll fetch our doctor and the patient and we're off to Hong Kong."

"Well, I've been thinking about this maneuver," Cat said, "but the magazine article doesn't tell me how to aim the plane. I mean somehow I must sight the target and keep it constantly in my view looking down over my left shoulder. Does this make sense to you Jefferies?"

"That little detail I'll leave to you to sort out on the first practice pickup. I'm sure after the first lift you'll have it nailed. We'll do our job to be sure there is plenty of slack in the line as they load the basket and when we get the radio signal that all is ready, we'll begin the lift. We do have a walkie talkie just for that purpose.

"Again Jefferies," Cat said, "You've thought of just about everything. I hope for your sake this little scheme of yours works. Please excuse me as I need to start my pre-flight checks." Turning to Larry Chen he continued, "We'll radio you on the company frequency when we have completed our practice run and are headed back."

"Good luck Cat. Piece of cake," Larry said as he gave him a big thumb up.

Cat gave Larry an evil eye look and started up the ladder into the cargo bay. As he came up the ladder he could see Lling Munai and Jefferies helper stowing some boxes. Jefferies was right behind him on the ladder. As he walked forward to the cockpit, he noticed that a row of passenger seats was installed up front, presumably for Jefferies and his pickup passengers. He shook his head, thinking that everything was just too tidy. Seems no detail had been omitted from Jefferies plan. Entering the cockpit he could see Trish in her seat going through the pre-flight checklist. Cat said nothing as he sat down and buckled himself in and put his headphones on. Lling appeared in the doorway.

"All ready Captain Cat," Lling said, "Cargo door closed and passengers are buckled in."

"Lling, call the tower and get taxi clearance," Cat said as Lling sat down at his radio station, buckled in and turned on his radio set.

"Miss Mathews have you completed the preflight checklist?" Cat asked, "And the walk around."

"Yes Captain," she replied handing him the checklist clipboard. Cat looked it over carefully, nodded and placed it beside him.

"Now I want you to start engines," Cat said, "It will be good practice. Prime them twice and be sure we are feathered. Crank her two times before turning on the ignition. I'll be watching."

She looked over and smiled and went through the engine start procedure. Soon both engines came to life in their normal noisy rumble fashion before settling down. She adjusted the throttle levers until both engines were purring perfectly and then pulled both back to the idle position.

"Well done Miss Mathews," he said, as he looked at the gages to be sure all was in order.

Looking out the window he could see Larry Chen and Jasmine standing by the hanger. She waved at him. A message came from Lling on the interphone that the 'Lucky Seven' was authorized to taxi. Time to get this over with, he thought to himself.

"This is MalSing seven taxing to 27 West," Cat said into his microphone after switching his radio to the tower frequency.

"MalSing seven," came the reply from the Changi Airfield tower controller, "proceed taxi 27 West and wait for final."

Cat then released the parking brakes, added some pitch to the propellers and moved the throttles forward until the *'Lucky Seven'* began crawling forward to the runway taxiway. Reaching the end he turned the plane until the C-46 pointed straight down the runway. He stepped on the brakes bringing the plane to a stop. He again feathered the propellers and ran the engines up and down.

"MalSing seven ready for takeoff," Cat spoke into the mike.

"Roger MalSing seven you are clear for takeoff 27 West." the tower controller replied.

"Miss Mathews," Cat barked into the interphone, "give me flaps 20."

Trish moved the flap control levers to the takeoff position, and looked out her window to be sure they were deployed on her side. Cat instinctively looked out his window to also confirm deployment. He pushed both throttles full forward, made sure the propeller pitch was perfect, adjusted the fuel mixture, looked over to Trish, who was looking at him and took his foot off the brakes. The *'Lucky Seven'*, with barely any load, leapt down the runway and into the afternoon air effortlessly.

"Flaps and wheels up," Cat ordered Trish on the interphone, as he pulled back the throttles and adjusted the propeller and mixture controls. She moved the flap levers which brought them back into flying position while simultaneously moving the landing gear up levers. Climbing, turning and banking through 1000 feet the *'Lucky Seven'* was already over the Straits of Johore and into Malaysia. He set a northeast course for Taman Sri Lalang near Kota Tinggi and settled back in his seat and stared out the windshield for a minute. Not a cloud could he see in the sky.

Chapter **12**

"Miss Mathews," Cat said, "take the controls and keep us on course and 5000 ft. I need to talk to Jefferies for a minute. Keep her steady as she goes!"

When she had the plane, Cat took his hands off his yoke, unbuckled and headed back to the cargo bay. He walked past Lling and grabbed the spare interphone headphones and mike off the hook on his way. Jefferies was sitting down next to his mechanic. As he approached, Jefferies unbuckled his seatbelt, stood up and stepped out into the aisle.

"Jefferies," Cat said. "We'll be in the practice area in a few minutes. Now are your men on the ground going to put out some smoke?"

"All taken care of Captain. When they hear us, or when I reach them on the walkie-talkie, they'll release the smoke bombs. You'll see them clearly."

"Now I'll spiral down slowly and make our circle tighter as I go down. Listen to my altitude countdown on these phones," he said as he handed them to Jefferies. "Plug them in near the cargo door. When we reach 750 ft, your winch cable should be on the ground. You can start reeling it out as soon as we get into our 30 degree bank. I'll try to keep her at that height. You tell me when the basket is on the way up and I'll take the plane up at the same time increasing the spiral until you have the basket inside. Then you give me the OK signal when the basket is on board and I'll straighten her out nice and level. When you have everything stowed we'll do the same thing again. Sound like a plan?"

"Captain, that should work perfectly," Jefferies said.

"Good. We've less than 2 minutes flight to the target area. I'll send Lling back when we are there to assist you as needed," he said.

"Excellent Captain McCoy," Jefferies said with a smile on his face as he turned to his assistant and gave him a nod to head back and get the winch gear ready. Both then proceeded to the back of the plane and put their harnesses on.

Cat returned to the cockpit and buckled in. He looked over at Trish and she seemed to be enjoying her new C-46 piloting experience. Cat pulled out the map with the practice area marked; looked at the instruments and his watch, and confirmed they were on course and about 2 minutes to the practice area. He put the map on the clipboard and sat back in his seat to quickly think things over before the maneuver would begin. The secret to banking the plane was to start high and wide, like at the top of a funnel, and then slowly corkscrew down to 750 feet. The diameter of the tight circle he would fly would be one-third to one-quarter mile.

"Take her down to 2000 feet and look for smoke," Cat said as she then pushed the yoke gently forward and down they went.

Switching on the interphone he instructed Lling to head to the back and help Jefferies.

"There's the smoke Cat," Trish pointed out as they approached overhead.

"OK, now let Cat take over from here," he said into the interphone. "Trish you keep the 30 degree bank as I work the pedals. Give me some flaps and throttle up. We're going to come close to a stall, but we'll have plenty of lift. Keep her at 120 knots. Nod to me that you understand."

Trish looked over and nodded.

"Good, now Jefferies are you listening,"

"Right here old boy," Jefferies replied.

"Get your winch ready as we're going to take her down at that 30 degree angle. And keep my man Lling from falling out,' Cat said.

Soon Cat spiraled down and had the *Lucky Seven'* in the tight bank with the ground smoke centered in his left eye as he twisted his head to the left as far as he could. Counting down into the interphone he shouted 900 feet, then 800 feet and then 750 ft. He had the big C-46 in the tightest banked circle he ever flew.

"Jefferies we're there," he said into the open interphone mike.

Over his shoulder he could see the winch cable and basket hitting the ground and men putting something in the basket and closing the top cage. Then the basket left the ground.

"Captain McCoy, you can increase your circle and bring her up," Jefferies said. "It should take less than 90 seconds for the basket to reach the door. All is going as planned."

Cat pushed the yoke out slowly to increase the circle, while Trish continued to maintain the 30 degree bank. In another minute Jefferies shouted into the interphone they had the basket. Cat then told Trish to level up and then take her back up to 2000 feet in a slow circle around the smoke. Jefferies appeared in the doorway with a smile on his face and patted Cat on the back of his shoulder.

"Splendid flying Captain McCoy and Miss Matthews," he said looking at both of them, "one more perfect pick up like that and we head for home. Well done, well done."

As Jefferies turned and returned to the cargo bay, Cat basked in the momentary praise, but knew he had to repeat his aerial acrobatics one more time today without a hitch and two more times tomorrow morning before the praise would be earned. He talked with Trish on the interphone about setting up the second lift and soon the 'Lucky Seven' was slowly descending in the ever tightening 30 degree circle. In less than fifteen minutes they had the second basket safe on board and were heading back to Changi field. The tires touched down on the runway and soon Trish was shutting off the engines in front of the MalSing Air Charter Service hanger. Start to finish they had less than two hours flying.

"Well done Trish," Cat said as he unbuckled and stood up. "Please complete the after landing checklist and paperwork, make sure Lling has this baby refueled and ready for our rescue and Hong Kong adventure tomorrow. We'll take off at 7 am sharp so be here by 6 am for preflight."

"Eye, eye Captain," she replied, "piece of cake!"

Cat just looked at her with the evil eye again and proceeded to the cargo bay where Larry Chen had come aboard to talk with Jefferies. Both were smiling and shaking hands and back slapping when an exhausted Cat approached. Lling and Jefferies man were stowing gear and inspecting the winch.

"Wonderful flying Captain McCoy," Jefferies said, "You clearly are the best pilot in Singapore."

Cat thanked him, but said to both men the real test would be tomorrow morning on the rescue. He excused himself and told them he would be ready for a 7 am takeoff in the morning and for all to be onboard at that time. With that, he climbed down the ladder and walked slowly into the pilot's ready room. Surprisingly Trish was right behind him with the flight paperwork. She handed it to Cat and disappeared in the loo. Shortly she reemerged with her two suitcases.

"Say, mind giving me a lift to my apartment," Trish asked Cat in a wonderfully soothing and relaxed tone.

"Sure, sure, just put your stuff in the Land Rover outside." he said, "I'll meet you there in a minute."

Trish walked out the door suitcases in hand as Cat took the paperwork into the office, where Jasmine seeing him jumped up from her desk, ran over and kissed him for the longest time before stepping back.

"Thanks Jasmine," Cat spoke softly, "I was only gone for two hours. You needn't worry about me ever."

"I know, but I do worry about you sometimes," she said.

"Listen, I'm exhausted and am heading home to crash. When I get back from Hong Kong, I want to talk with you about 'us'," Cat whispered to her. She smiled and nodded and took the paperwork from his hand. Cat kissed her again, turned and walked back into the hangar with that glowing grin back on his face. Soon he was outside and climbing into the Land Rover where Trish was waiting. He turned the motor on and started to back up.

"Ok Miss Trish, where too," he asked as he stopped, put the 'Rover' into 1st gear and charged out of the parking area onto the access road.

"963 Upper Change Road," she replied.

Upon hearing that Cat slammed on the brakes and pulled off to the side of the Road and faced Trish.

"That's where I live," he said, "What's this all about."

"Oh. Larry Chen arranged an apartment for me. He said it was very convenient and you wouldn't mind giving me a lift to and from work." she said a little perplexed.

"Oh he did, did he," Cat tossed out in an elevated tone with a look of perplexed amazement on his face. "Well fine howdy do for the Cat man."

Cat slammed the shifter in first gear and the Land Rover leaped back onto the road and got up to speed. His apartment was a five minute ride at normal speeds, but he parked the Rover and had the ignition off in front of '963' in under three minutes. Trish was all white knuckled in her seat and trying to compose herself when Cat leapt out, slammed the door and very discourteously left her sitting in the 'Rover.' He climbed up the stairs to apartment 3C, turned the key in the lock and cautiously walked in closing the door behind him. He continued on to the sofa, crashed down and was taken immediately into a deep sleep by the God Morpheus.

Chapter **13**

The knock on Cat's door got louder and louder in his ears. His eyes opened in the dark and he slowly stood up and headed toward the door. The knocking continued. He flipped on the light switch and opened the door to see a stunning blond woman staring at him catching him completely off guard. As he refocused his eyes he could see it was Trish in a low cut summer dress and sandals holding two beers.

"May I please come in," she asked as Cat continued to stare at her without saying anything.

"Well," she said again.

"Of course," Cat replied trying to wake up. "Come on in."

"Here. This will help you wakeup. She said handing him the opened beer. "I want to clear the air before tomorrow. Not sure what's going on here, but if I'm unwelcome, please say so now, so I can pack and move on.

Cat was taken completely off guard by her comments, and tried desperately to get back to full consciousness.

"Come on out to the balcony Trish to talk," he motioned to her as they moved outside and sat down facing the Changi air field in the distance with its rotating beacon and blue field lights in clear sight. He tugged on the cold beer a few swallows that helped him wake up and relax at the same time.

"Trish, I want to apologize for my crazy driving getting you here. I can't explain this, but I haven't been in control of anything these past 24 hours. Absolutely nothing. More unexpected things have happened to me and more crazy decisions have I made, and more changes have occurred, including you, than the ole Cat could handle. Guess I just blew in the 'Rover.' Sorry. I now realize I was just taking everything out on you and shouldn't have. Of course you still have the job, and I still want to teach you all about the C-46 and Southeast Asia. It's just, it's just you are a beautiful woman, as well as an accomplished pilot. I mean you are overloaded with brains and beauty at the same time. I mean, I mean," he stumbled on while incoherent words kept tumbling out of his mouth. Trish was smiling profusely, laughed and clearly enjoying his verbal performance. "We are equals in the flying game...or should be professionally, and that's the way I want to keep it...professional..."

Time to shut up Cat, he said to himself...Shut up and have another pull on your beer.

"Cat," she said with a wry smile on her face trying to hold back her laughter again, "I can understand how you feel. Sorry for all the changes, but they are just that...changes...everything changes all the time. Nothing you can do to prevent changes, or

71

slow them down, even if you tried. I think you are handling things very well."

"Look Trish, let's start over right now. I promise not to be a jerk…ok??

"Apology accepted Cat," as he reached over and their bottles clinked.

"Now tell me a little about yourself," he said, "tell me how you got here."

"Cat, it's a long story, but I'll keep it short," she said, "I began to fly back in England in 1942 and got my license. My Dad was in the RAF at the time, and flew the Wellington bomber on nighttime raids over Germany. I was just 19 in 1943 and wanted to enlist in the RAF myself, but they had a ban on women in flight crews. That old British chivalrous thing or something. Anyway, my Daddy arranged for me to take flight training as a ferry pilot with the Air Transport Auxiliary, which was the most exciting time of my life up to that point. After a years training, and we put in 12 hour days, seven days a week, I started out flying fighters from the factories in England to various airfields around Britain. I loved the hurricanes and spits, so much power and speed. I had an accident, you know, when one day the hydraulics went out and the landing gear wouldn't go down on my spit. Even the manual crank would not work, so it was a wheels up landing for me. Something you talk about and practice in your head, but having to break a brand new plane made me want to cry. I never even thought about my own safety, only the thought that my spit was on the fritz and we were going in. Anyway, they talked me down and I brought that plane in without much damage at all. They congratulated me on the gentle landing…Oh boy!"

"Then they assigned me to twin engine training and the next thing I was flying American aircraft from Canada to England, with another gal. Her name was Gwen Collins, and we were and still are super close friends. She was two years older and more experienced at twin engine flying than I was at the time, but being the co-pilot suited me just fine. The hops to Labrador, Iceland, Ireland and Scotland became our life for over a year. We flew C-47 Dakotas, B-25's, B-26's, Boston's, you name it just as fast as we could turn around. And then the war in Europe was over. Within days of the end in May 1945, I was back home without a job and without a clue on what to do for work, as the men were going to return soon and take all the jobs. After almost a year, in January or February of 1946 my family home, and England, became very small to me and with my Dad's help again, I was hired by Canadian Express Airlines in Edmonton, Canada. When I got there, I found they wanted me to be a stewardess, of all things, me an accomplished woman pilot, not unlike Amelia Earhart. Ha!" She said, as they both chuckled.

"I showed the general manager I had over 1,000 hours twin engine time in my log book, mostly in C-47's and I needed to fly. Well, Mr. Neff, that was his name. Well Mr. Neff said I had to start as a stewardess because there were no women airline pilots in Canada. So did I want the job or not? I remember looking at him in the eyes for the longest time. My brain was racing trying to decide what to do, when my mouth opened and I said 'Yes, Mr. Neff, I want the job.' So I was a stewardess, but the boys up front knew I wanted to fly and every chance I got, they let me take over the right seat. In fact, I had more flight time than several of the new pilots they hired fresh from his Majesty's Canadian Air forces...."

"Another year went by rapidly. Still I couldn't get officially into the cockpit of the airline and I then began to look around for anything else; well the frozen north beckoned and I changed jobs and began flying cargo in DC-3's up the northwest territories and into Alaska. No stewardess needed on these runs! This lasted a couple of years and I just got fed up with the cold and snow and read an ad in one of the trade publications about flying jobs in Australia. Well, I was on my way. This was early in 1950. Well, I got to Sidney, via hitching rides on anything that would fly that way. It's amazing what this kisser can accomplish when all else fails. Are you bored yet?" she said to Cat.

"Trish, this is exciting, tell me more," he said.

"Well in Sydney I walked into the air charter company and asked to apply for the job. They laughed and said the job was filled, but they needed a trained stewardess, so here we go again. Am I a sucker or what? The mouth said yes again, but the brain was saying kiss my ass!" she said, as Cat was smiling and loving every minutes of her story.

"So I became a stewardess again. We flew Dakota's across the Australian outback from Sydney to Perth. We'd land in the middle of nowhere and people would be waiting to get on the plane. I did this for about a year when John, one of the pilots, got a little too frisky with me on a stopover and I had to, let's say, cool him off as he wasn't for me. Unfortunately, and while I'm no prude, I knew this wasn't going to work. Making it worse, he was one of the owner's sons and was married. It all went down hill from then on."

"Next I went to Darwin and was hired by an air charter company as copilot flying up to Borneo, New Guinea and Indonesia. I made a few stops here in Singapore and noticed the MalSing name, but paid it no mind. Needless to say the Darwin based job ended when I came here. And I was glad, as it was so God damn hot there. I couldn't stand it anymore. It seems my boss at Aussie Air knew Mr. Chen. In fact they had known each other during the war. He wired him that he had an excellent pilot available and here I am. The end!"

"Excellent tale Trish," Cat said when he heard knocking at the door. Both looked at each other.

"I'll be right back, he said as he got up and headed to the unlocked door, just as Jasmine walked in.

"Hello flyboy," she said as she rushed up to him with arms out ready to jump into his, but at the last moment she saw Trish standing in the balcony door behind him walking into the room in her slinky dress. Jasmine's face changed immediately as she stared at Trish and instantly became all business like, steely eyed and composed. Before he could say anything Jasmine began to speak.

"Oh Hello Miss Matthews," she said calmly stepping to the side staring at Trish and trying her best to control her emotions. Then she turned back facing Cat. "Cat, my father wanted me to drop off your approved flight plan for tomorrow clear through to Hong Kong. I see you two are getting to know each other. Well I'll be leaving now," she said as she handed the flight plan folder to Cat. "I don't want to interrupt your get together."

Cat stood there frozen saying nothing as Jasmine said goodbye to both of them, turned around and hastily headed out the door closing it behind her. Tears were forming in her eyes as she raced down the stairs; jump into her fathers car and drove away.

Cat continued to stand in the middle of his apartment, holding the beer in one hand and flight plan in the other as Trish walked up beside him. She knew immediately what had happened and sensing this was an awkward moment for Cat, decided to leave and return to her apartment as well.

"Listen Cat," she said, "I must go. See you tomorrow morning in the Land Rover at 5:45 am."

"Yes," said Cat, "see you in the Rover. Good night Trish."

Trish left the apartment and now Cat was all alone standing there wondering what had just happened. The woman that he loved gone with hurt feelings and nothing he could say or do to change any of this now. He reflected again on all the changes in his life in the past twenty-four hours, and for the first time felt he had woman problems without doing anything to deserve it. Would this day ever end, he thought to himself?

"Women," he said quietly out loud as he headed into his bedroom and crashed on his bed. "What's next?"

Chapter **14**

Trish was waiting in the front seat of the Land Rover when Cat opened the driver's door and got in.

"Good morning Miss Mathews," he said formally as he turned the key in the ignition.

"Good morning Captain McCoy," she replied.

Cat proceeded to the Changi Airfield hangar without saying a word. They parked and both walked into the hangar and pilots ready room. He could see that Lling was already working on the plane over on the tarmac and getting her ready.

"Trish, please put the joe on in the pantry and bring me a cup when its done," he said, "and then lets go over the flight plan."

She nodded and went to make the coffee. Cat sat at the table and unfolded Jefferies map where the big 'X' marked the rescue pickup spot east of Labis in the Endau Mountains and studied it. Soon Trish appeared by his side with two hot cups of joe.

"I didn't think you Limey's liked coffee," he said humorously as she handed him the cup.

"Some of us do that have hung around enough Americans as I have," she said in good spirits.

"Now Trish look here," he said pointing to the map as she listened and sipped her cup of joe. "I hope we're not going to have much fog on this side of the mountain when we arrive. I'll ask Jefferies if they can put flares out to mark the spot in case we can't see the ground. Worst case we'll have to fly around until the sun burns the ground fog off. Otherwise, the weather report is CAVU all day. We'll use the same procedure we did yesterday. You keep the 30 degree angle and handle the airspeed and flaps, and I'll bring her down in our tight circle. After the Doctor and our patient are on board, we'll fly to Saigon and then on the Hong Kong. Check with Lling and be sure our tanks are topped off. Any questions?"

"Sounds like a plan Captain," she said. "I'll go out to the plane and begin the pre-flight checks."

"Trish, please take our map bag with you over there, and be sure we have lots of sandwiches and drinks onboard. And fill my thermos up with coffee if you don't mind," he asked politely.

"Roger Cap," she replied while heading to the panty and flight line.

Jefferies and Larry Chen walked into the pilots ready room.

"Good morning Cat," Larry Chen said in his usual jovial tone. "What a great day for a rescue. No?"

Cat greeted them both and said everything was ready for take-off at 7 am. He asked Jefferies if they could put flares out in the pickup area, as there could be ground fog. Jefferies assured him the pickup up area will be completely visible from the air, and that his men up there on the ground have already been instructed to put red flares out when they hear us overhead. Cat was amazed again that Jefferies had thought of everything. It was all just too perfect. After going over the flight plan and pickup procedure again with Jefferies and Larry Chen, Cat excused himself and headed out to the 'Lucky Seven' as dawn was breaking. They followed behind talking and laughing with smiles on both their faces. Cat strode briskly to the plane and did his normal walk around, when Lling Munai walked up beside him.

"Captain Cat," strange thing about yesterday," he said.

"What do you mean Lling," he replied.

"Well, they pulled up two sacks in each basket haul and placed them all into one of those steel boxes and locked it up. Their mechanic Beng slept on the plane last night. He told me he had no other place to go. I closed the cargo bay door with him onboard," he replied.

"Yes that seems strange, but these guys have a reason for everything," Cat said. "Not to worry Lling, I'll ask them about that. Are we ready to go? he asked.

"Yes Captain. All ready with fuel tanks topped off."

"Excellent Lling," he said. "Now get our weather report, taxi clearance and Jefferies on board."

Lling walked toward the hangar as Cat headed to the cargo bay ladder and climbed on board. The Malaysian Oil Company mechanic Beng was sitting on the steel box as Cat walked into the cockpit where Trish was seated working on the pre-flight checklist. He sat down in his pilots seat, buckled in and turned to Trish.

79

"Something strange going on here Lling tells me. They locked up those bags of rocks we lifted yesterday in one of those steel boxes bolted to the floor. Seems their man babysat them all night," he exclaimed.

Trish turned and faced him.

"That is curious," she replied, "but seems they can carry whatever they want on this trip."

"You're right, of course. Not my problem or concern," he said. "Now are we all checked out?"

"All checked out. Just need the weather report and we can get this over with," she said as Lling popped his head in the cockpit.

"All passengers on board. Cargo door closed. We ready to taxi," Lling said as he handed the weather report and taxi orders to Trish.

"Great Lling. Buckle up and let's get this mission over," he said.

In another 15 minutes Cat was standing on the brakes with the *Lucky Seven's* engines straining at full power staring down runway 27 West. He slipped his foot off the brakes and began the takeoff roll. Soon the C-46 was up into the morning sunlight and headed North, North West to the Endau Mountains. Again, Cat popped out of his seat after giving control to Trish. He told Lling to go back and help the Malaysian Oil man and walked back to see Jefferies, who also stood up and stepped into the isle as Cat approached.

"Twenty minutes to the rescue site," Cat called out over the drone of the engines.

"Sorry Captain, there has been a change of plans. Here is your new course and directions," Jefferies said as he handed Cat a map with a line drawn to Rangoon Burma and then to Bombay, India.

"What do you mean change of plans? What about the rescue of your geologist," Cat asked in an inquisitive and questioning voice.

"Oh, he died yesterday. No need to pick up the body. They'll truck him out. But we do have cargo to take to Bombay," Jefferies stated matter of fact very nonchalantly.

"Look Jefferies, the only place we're going is back to Singapore," Cat said

"Sorry ole boy. We're going to Rangoon," he said as he pulled out a Colt 45 automatic pistol from his pocket and aimed it at Cat's chest. "I must insist. Now let's go back to the cockpit to change course," as he motioned for Cat to turn around.

"You'll never get away with this Jefferies," Cat shouted standing his ground.

"Don't you worry about it Captain. I already have," he exclaimed. "Listen up. You set course for Rangoon to refuel then on to Bombay and everybody lives a long life. Simple as that."

Cat looked over his shoulder and could see Jefferies man Beng holding a revolver on Lling. He knew gun fire on planes was really bad as people will die and the killing only starts a snowball of unfortunate and deadly outcomes for all. Too risky to play superman with a 45 caliber pointed at your chest he thought.

"OK Jefferies, Rangoon and Bombay it is. No problem. You chartered the plane so we'll take you where you want to go," Cat said.

"Smart thinking Captain," Jefferies replied while still motioning with his gun for Cat to move, "Everybody wins.

Everybody lives. Now up to the cockpit we go for a chat with missy."

Cat had his own 38 revolver in the map bag, but it was no match for what was facing him. As Cat sat down in his seat Trish looked over and then glanced back at Jefferies and then at the gun pointed at Cat's head. Cat turned to Trish.

"New course heading Bombay via Rangoon Trish," Cat shouted taking over the controls. "Chart the course and advise fuel."

With those instructions, Trish reached behind her and dragged the map bag out and began looking for new maps. She saw the 38 revolver, looked up to Cat, but he just shook his head no. She pulled out the maps and placed them on her clipboard and began plotting the course. Several minutes passed by.

"Five hours to Rangoon and fuel aok. 1184 miles," she shouted out to Cat so Jefferies could here. "Adjust course to three five zero. Maintain speed two zero zero."

Cat made the heading changes, adjusted the throttles and engaged the autopilot.

"No radio traffic until we get landing clearance at Rangoon and no funny business Captain, or your co-pilot may have an accident," Jefferies said as he settled down into Lling's radioman's seat with the gun pointed at Cat.

In the cargo bay, Malaysian Oil Company mechanic Beng was ordering Lling at gunpoint to begin disassembly of the winch apparatus and everything else they had brought on board. In little over an hour everything was piled near the cargo bay doors - winch assemblies, electric motors, cables, battery boxes, and seats. As the plane headed up the west coast of Malaysia and now finally over water Lling was ordered to open the inside cargo bay door and toss everything out piece by piece. In another fifteen minutes nothing remained in the cargo bay, except the one steel box. The inner cargo bay door was closed. Lling was then ordered to tell Cat on the interphone that the cargo bay was empty and to pass that on to Jefferies.

"Jefferies, the cargo bay is empty whatever that means," Cat shouted to Jefferies who grinned and nodded while still pointing the gun at Cat.

The flight to Rangoon was on schedule and uneventful, except for the high tension, drama and fear associated with having a hand gun pointed at your head. Other than that the flight was a milk run for Cat. With Forty five minutes till landing in Rangoon Cat turn to face Jefferies.

"Jefferies ole boy, I need to call Rangoon for landing clearance to refuel," Cat shouted.

"Go ahead and make arrangement to stop for fuel only. Careful what you say Captain," Jefferies shouted back.

Cat switched to the Rangoon Airport frequency and keyed his mike.

"Rangoon, this is MalSing Seven from Singapore on charter Bombay requesting refueling clearance, Bukit Air Services. Landing in 30 minutes." he said.

"MalSing Seven, hello, good afternoon. Clearance granted to refuel," the Rangoon air controller acknowledged.

"How are we doing on fuel?" Cat asked looking over at Trish.

"One hour fifty," she replied looking up from her clipboard navigational charts.

Jefferies stood up and walked into the cockpit where both Cat and Trish could hear him. He said no one would get off the plane except his man Beng to refuel, check the aircraft and cable Indian Air control of their flight plan and Bombay ETA. The MalSing flight crew could go back into the cargo bay for a leg stretch when they landed. He asked them politely not to try anything funny, as this wasn't really a hijacking, just a change of course. He reiterated no harm would come to any of Cat's crew if all cooperated in getting them to Bombay.

The 'Lucky Seven' landed in "Rangoon, refueled, and was in the air headed to Bombay in less than an hour. Their new flight plan took them 1500 miles due West over the Bay of Bengal. Trish estimated the flying time between six and seven hours at 225 mph. Everything depended on the headwinds at their 15,000 ft flying altitude. Land fall would be in four hours and 900 miles from Rangoon. Things were loosening up on the flight as they journeyed across the water. Jefferies put his gun down on the table as Lling passed out sandwiches and refreshment to all five souls on board. Jefferies allowed Cat and Trish to each get up and walk back alone to the rear cargo bay lavatory unescorted, however he always kept his gun on the one flying the plane.

They encountered some turbulence crossing the Bay of Bengal and many cloud formations, but made Indian landfall on schedule. Cat had to make radio contact with the nearest large airport in India as he crossed the coast and he chose Hyderabad. His radio call was brief confirming destination Bombay. After several minutes, the air controller acknowledged their registered flight and gave clearance to proceed to Bombay's Dum Dum airport. They expected to land just before dusk and three time zones difference from Singapore. Interestingly, Jefferies wanted to know their exact position every 15 minutes after landfall for some reason. When they were one hour away from Bombay, it became apparent.

"Captain McCoy," Jefferies said while standing over Cat with the revolver at his side and not pointed at him, "Another change of plan. I want you to set course for Poona, near Bombay a little south marked here on this map. A temporary diversion and then you continue on to Bombay."

Jefferies handed Cat the map with Poona circled and further explained their destination was an abandoned US Air Force base on the north east outskirts of town. He instructed Cat to just fly in a around circle around the air base at 500 ft and look for flares and smoke as before. He said they would not be landing. Cat looked at Trish and she quickly recalculated their route and distance and ETA. They would have just 45 minutes fuel remaining after reaching Poona, enough to make Bombay, but no more.

"Look Jefferies," Cat exclaimed, "We're cutting this real close on fuel. How long must we linger around?"

"Two minutes tops while we drop our cargo and then we're off to holiday in Bombay," he jovially said looking at the two of them. "Just look for the smoke, circle and we'll do the rest.

Back in the cargo bay, Beng unlocked the steel box and both he and Lling pulled the four heavy sacks out of the box. Each was put into another heavy burlap bag, strapped with a parachute attached to each. All four bags were placed by the inner cargo bay door which was now open.

As they approached Poona, Cat brought the plane down to hunt for the air strip. It flashed by almost hidden by the jungle overgrowth that was trying to reclaim it from both sides. Jefferies was looking out the window and keying his walkie talkie when it squawked back at with a voice saying something to the effect…'see you loud and clear flares started.' Cat and Trish could now see the smoke and red flares burning in the middle of one abandoned runway. They began circling at 500 feet. As they approached the air strip Lling and Beng pushed the four sacks out and deployed the parachutes. They fluttered to the ground near the air strip. Now Beng removed two more parachutes from the steel box and then had Lling unbolt the steel box from the floor and toss it out of the plane too.

"Mission accomplished," Jefferies told Cat and Trish. "Now bring her up to 3000 ft over the airfield and continue circling. When you reach altitude let me know on the interphone."

"Mind telling me Jefferies what our cargo is," Cat asked

"Sorry ole boy. Can't do that for your safety, Jefferies said, "The less you all know the better. However, here's a little bonus in appreciation of your flying skills. Now let me know on the interphone when you get to 3000 ft."

With that, Jefferies handed Cat ten gold coins and exited the cockpit. He closed the inner cockpit door and locked it so Cat and Trish could not get out. In 5 more minutes, as instructed, Cat told Jefferies on the interphone they were at 3000 ft over the airport. Cat thought that when they landed in Bombay Jefferies and his accomplice could escape, but for how long after Cat reported what had happened to the Bombay police. Anyway all this would be over in less than an hour. Lling rushed into the cockpit.

"Captain Cat, Lling said, "They all gone. Jumped out. Plane empty. We alone."

Cat looked out the window and could see two parachutes just landing on the ground.

"Trish, get us to Dum Dum pronto," he said as he got up after handing her the controls and went back to the cargo bay with Lling. It was completely empty. Nothing remained. Nothing. Cat was having a hard time understanding what he was seeing and what had just happened. Returning to the cockpit he could hear Trish talking with Bombay Dum Dum airport for immediate landing clearance due to low fuel. When asked by the tower why they were late she replied they had to fly around some weather. Cat buckled in and they landed smoothly pulling into the air cargo hanger area near the fixed base operator and shut down the engines. All just sat in their seats saying nothing. Cat was confused. Trish was visibly shaken. Lling just sat there shaking his head. After what seemed like a long time, but in reality was only a minute, Cat composed himself and looked at Trish.

"Anybody want a drink?" Cat asked in a smiling face, "I'm buying."

Everyone jumped up from their seats, gathered their overnight bags and exited the empty plane. They all walked to the FBO office where Cat ordered a taxi to take them to the Intercontinental Bombay Hotel. Cat told the office staff to refuel and service the plane for a 7 am Singapore return departure tomorrow. Soon the taxi arrived and the exhausted crew climbed in and just looked out the windows at the early Bombay evening. Arriving at the hotel, they checked in. Cat instructed Trish and Lling to meet him in the bar in thirty minutes for a crew meeting and all went to their rooms.

Chapter **15**

While freshening up in his room, Cat knew he had been used for something apparently illegal, but what he wasn't sure. The ten gold sovereigns in his pocket were also a strange piece of the puzzle, but where did they fit in? The entire rescue story from start to finish was just too fantastic for anyone to believe, much less the Indian authorities, and impossible to prove too. Cleaned up, Cat walked into the hotel bar where his crew was waiting at a nearby table and apparently on their second drink. After pleasantries and finishing his second gin and tonic, Cat called the meeting to order.

"Great to be alive isn't it," he started out. "I wanted to talk to you both about the events today while everything is fresh in our minds. I have decided what to do and hope you all agree, concur or at least understand. First I don't want to go to the Indian Authorities with our fantastic story, and not a shred of evidence. I am not even sure if a crime has been committed. We've just been victim to a massive change of course from the guys who chartered the plane in the first place. So I vote we all get some sleep and fly back to Singapore in the morning. There I will fully brief Larry Chen and see if we should go to the police there with our story. Now, I have these ten gold sovereigns Jefferies, or whatever his name is, gave me. I think we should keep them for ourselves as souvenirs. All in favor raise your glasses and take a drink."

All three raised their glasses and finished their drinks, slamming them down on the table at the same time and then all began laughing. Cat handed three coins to Trish, three to Lling.

"Hey, what about the fourth coin," Trish asked in a wonderfully buzzed expression.

"Oh that is for Larry or the Singapore police," Cat replied. "I don't know about you, but I am exhausted. So see you all at 5 am in the lobby."

And with that Cat, Trish and Lling all stood up and went wearily, but in good spirits to their rooms. While on his way, Cat stopped at the front desk and wrote out a telegram addressed to Larry Chen:

LARRY CHEN, MALSING AIR CHARTER,
CHANGI, SINGAPORE. LEAVING
BOMBAY MONDAY MORNING FOR
CHANGI STOP. ALL SAFE ARRIVAL
EARLY EVENING STOP. WILL EXPLAIN
ALL ON RETURN CAPTAIN MCCOY STOP.

Chapter **16**

It was just after 5 am Monday when Cat and his crew jumped into their taxi for the journey to Bombay Dum Dum airport. Lling sat next to the driver and Trish joined Cat in the back seat. They were partially refreshed from their sleep, but all knew a grueling day of flight was ahead of them. It was still pitch black outside as the taxi pulled away from the brightly lit hotel entrance. Trish turned to Cat, who was staring out the window.

"Cat," she said, "I have gone over everything in my mind and everything appeared legitimate until that pistol was pointed at your head. Explain this to me. The preparation on their part was extensive. They spared no money, overlooked no detail. Everything happened at the precise time. Getting whatever was in those sacks to India was the purpose of all this, but surely don't they expect us to go to the police. Isn't that part of their plan too? And if we do go to the police, will we be dragged into something deeper?"

Trish continued to talk. Cat listened, but said nothing as the driver deftly maneuvered his vehicle through the busy and crowded Bombay streets even at this time of the morning. As he looked out the window at the passing stores and restaurants lit up by the occasional street light he was amazed. If anything the British did during the RAJ they laid out these Bombay streets in some reasonable sense where they could. Then Cat stopped listening to Trish and completely turned off everything, the taxi, the drive, the city sites and smells, everything as he momentarily withdrew for a little inner peace time to allow his subconscious to advise him on his next course of action. Cat's mind drifted back to the war when he just arrived in India and went to Bombay the first time to pick-up a brand new DC-3 for 'Hump' duty. He remembered he had a 24 hour pass and explored all the streets of Bombay, mostly on foot. The taxi drive was bringing back the sights, sounds and smells of this magical city he first experienced years ago. What was his name, oh yes Sargent Shay of the British Army, who he befriended in a local bar and they both explored Bombay together. He explained the 'Raj' to him, how India was a British colony since 1858 then, but now have been a free state since 1947 when Gandi and his non-violent movement set his people free. Cat harbored these wonderful feelings of Bombay inside him, its warm and colorful people and customs, which he learned later were completely different from his duty station in Assam. So much to discover in India and so little time he thought. His mind drifted back to 1952 and a bump in the road shook him most of the way back to full consciousness. Then it all came to him in a flash and so did everything else, the taxi ride, the traffic, noise, the sweet smell of Bombay in the early morning and Trish's words in his ear.

"Are you listening to me? Cat, are you ok? Cat, Cat, what's wrong?" she said as he slowly turned toward her and looked her straight in the eyes.

"This is only the beginning and of what I don't know," Cat told Trish. "And when will it be over, I don't know. But one thing is clear. We have been played hard Trish. Everybody has been played hard. But the game, the game is what puzzles me, as it should you. We don't know the game we are playing and whatever we do about this it's still part of the game. Their game! The good news, we are safe, sound and alive and heading home with three gold coins in our pocket, so whatever the game we are just paid pawns, but I would sure like to find out the bigger story here."

"I think you have it right Cat," she said.

"We'll sort this out further when we get back," he said, "now let's just focus on getting home safely."

The taxi continued to the airport with all the occupants silently sitting in the dark, where they have been for the past twenty-four hours. The 'Lucky Seven' with its lucky crew flew home in record time enjoying strong westerly tailwinds and arrived back at Changi field just before 7 pm Monday night. As Trish turned off the twin ignition switches the giant 16 ft propellers of the C-46 came to a well deserved rest. Home at last. Greeting them as they climbed down the cargo bay ladder was Larry Chen and Jasmine. The other MalSing ground crew standing behind them immediately began servicing and inspecting the C-46 after its long journey.

"Cat, Miss Matthews and Lling…. welcome home," Larry said looking at each of them in turn and shaking their hands. Jasmine stood at his side only looking at Cat. "Thanks for brief radio call explaining some of your adventure. Can we go into my office and get to the details please? I've some refreshment waiting for you."

"Okay boss, but can we keep it short," Cat said talking to Larry, but looking at Jasmine, "I think we are all suffering from mission fatigue and need some rest."

"Okay Cat, bring crew to office in five minutes. We talk fast," he said turning around and walking toward the hangar. Trish and Lling followed slowly behind Larry, leaving Cat and Jasmine standing alone on the tarmac, except for the five mechanics buzzing around them working on the '*Lucky Seven*'.

"I am sorry for jumping to conclusions Saturday night in your apartment," Jasmine said, "totally wrong of me. And after daddy tells me you had a gun pointed to your head by that Malaysian Oil Company man, and all the danger you were in, it made me think what is important, and that is our being together."

"I thought of you every minute, as well," he said smiling and staring fondly at her face. "We'll be together someday soon. It's just going to be trouble explaining 'us' to Larry. How will he take this? I know the rules around town."

"You leave the 'right time' to talk with him to me," she said wanting to jump into his arms, but holding back in her cool, sultry manner.

"Jasmine," he said, walking up and taking her hand for an instant, "that's fine. You tell me when. Now your father is waiting for us. We better go in."

They both walked slowly into the hangar bantering back and forth about the flight and eventually walked into Larry's private office where everyone was waiting. Trish and Lling were munching on sandwiches and having some tea.

"Good, now we can get our meeting going," Larry started out, "Now you say after take off Sunday morning Jefferies put a gun to your head and announced a course change to Bombay? And then his man, with Lling here's help, dumped all the winch equipment into the ocean? And then he pushed four sacks out of the plane southeast of Bombay? And then they both parachuted to the ground?

"In a nutshell Larry that's it," Cat said munching on his own sandwich and continuing to look at Trish and Lling, "Any of you guys want to add anything to the story?"

"No, that's pretty much it, Trish said.

"Crazy day," said Lling.

"Oh, one more thing Larry," Cat said, reaching into his pocket and tossing the gold sovereign onto Larry's desk, "We all got our souvenir of the mission, now here is yours. Jefferies gave us a few of these for a bonus."

Larry picked up the gold one oz sovereign in his hand and looked at it closely flipping it over and over. He immediately came to the same conclusion as Cat that his air charter service had been duped and used for some illegal activity and that gold was perhaps at the bottom of it. He knew that the price of gold in India was triple the world standard of British £12.5 per ounce, however, there have been no recent news reports of missing or stolen gold in Singapore and nothing in the quantity Cat estimated they tossed out of the 'Lucky Seven'. He didn't want to be considered an accomplice in any of this if inquiries were ever made. If there was something illegal in all this and he didn't report it, after accepting that tidy charter fee, it could mean real trouble. And if he goes to the authorities, they probably wouldn't believe a word of this, but at least it would be on record leaving the police just as puzzled as he. He placed the coin down on the desk and looked up at everyone staring at him.

"I see bad things in future if we don't report this to Singapore Police," he said looking around the faces in front of him. "I'll call and get an appointment downtown tomorrow at headquarters. Cat and Trish, you will accompany me and tell story and give this coin to them. I'll telephone you with the time. Cat you can drive Miss Mathews. Now good night to you all."

Larry reached across his desk and handed the gold sovereign back to Cat and told him to keep the coin until tomorrow. Everyone stood up and walked out of the office. Cat told Lling to take the day off and then turned to Jasmine, looked her lovingly in the eyes and said good night. She blew him a kiss. He then turned and walked out the hangar door to the parking area where Trish was waiting clearly exhausted. They both got in the Land Rover and headed to 963 Upper Changi Road for some well deserved rest. This time driving so slowly it took twice the normal drive time.

Chapter **17**

"Please come in and sit down," Inspector Barton Musk, age 50, of the Singapore police said waving Larry Chen, Cat and Trish into his office on the second floor of police headquarters. It was 10 am Tuesday morning. Handshakes and pleasantries were made as everyone sat down. Inspector Musk was having a hard time taking his eyes off Trish, but finally pulled them away and began. "Mr. Chen, you told me over the phone of some suspicious activity by a company that chartered one of your planes, The Malaysian Oil Exploration Co. Ltd., and a Mr. John Jefferies. Is that correct?"

"Yes Inspector," Larry replied, "they paid for an emergency air evacuation to Hong Kong for seriously injured geologist."

"And you say they outfitted your plane with a 'winch apparatus' and hauled up some sacks in Malaysia. Then the next day while airborne this Mr. Jefferies pointed a gun to the pilots heads and forced them to fly to Bombay versus Hong Kong.

And while en route tossed out the apparatus and shortly before landing they pushed some sacks on parachutes out of the plane and then both oil company men bailed out," he said reading from his telephone notes on his tablet.

"Exactly so," Larry said with a muted smile on his face, "Then my crew here flew right back to Singapore and reported this to me. My Captain McCoy has something for you."

Cat stood up and handed the gold sovereign to Inspector Musk who looked at it for a moment and placed it down on his desk.

"Inspector, the man named Jefferies handed this coin to me just before he parachuted out saying this was a bonus for a flying job well done," Cat said, "He kept his gun on me and my crew until he jumped.

"This is a very interesting story, but from what you say, I don't see any crime here as no one was injured, they chartered the plane from you anyway, and we don't know what was dropped from the plane. Mr. Chen here says the weight was close to 250 lbs per sack. I doubt they were filled with gold coins like this one. Trust me when I say there are no reports of stolen gold in that type of quantity anywhere in the world," the Inspector intoned and continued. "However, I will take your information and make routine inquires and let you know if anything turns up. We'll just file this under suspicious activity until we know more. Now Captain, can you describe this Jefferies fellow and his associate."

"Jefferies was about my age," Cat said, "mid thirties, mustache, six feet tall, very rugged, reddish hair and Australian sounding. His man named Beng was younger, Malaysian, dark hair and never spoke."

"Miss Matthews," he asked looking at her very closely, "Were you harmed in anyway?

"No, just frightened by having that pistol pointed at me," She said sharply noticing the Inspector tying to undress her with his eyes before glancing back at his desktop.

"Mr. Chen, how did they pay you?" the Inspector asked not looking up at him and continuing to write on his tablet.

"They pay in cash last Friday," Larry replied, "I put in bank that day,"

"Fine. That's about it for now," the Inspector said looking up at Larry, Trish and Cat facing him. "I would like to keep this coin for now and will return it to you at your offices in a day or so with a follow-up on all this. Thank you for stopping by."

With that, they all stood up, shook hands again, and Larry, Trish and Cat walked out of the Inspectors office and headed to the stairs. Behind them Inspector Musk came to his door looking at the disappearing Miss Mathews, while pointing to a man sitting behind a desk across the isle and waived him over.

"Sargent Wong, I want you to find out all you can on the Malaysian Oil Exploration Co. Ltd, and an Aussie named John Jefferies," he said, "I need this pronto Sargent and here, find out what you can about this gold coin," as he flipped the coin into the air and Wong grabbed it in his fist.

Inspector Musk returned to his desk, tore off the two pages of notes he had just taken and placed them in a folder marked 'Follow-up & Type."

Chapter **18**

"Oh hello Sir. May I help you?" Jasmine said as she looked up to a handsome man wearing a blue suit and tie staring down at her in the MalSing office accompanied by a British Army officer. It was Tuesday early in the afternoon.

"Yes please. Miles Atwater, Hong Kong and Shanghai Bank to see Mr. Chen about a charter," he said smiling at Jasmine while handing her his business card. "And this is Lieutenant McKnight."

She stood and walked into her father's office and in a few seconds emerged and walked up to them.

"Mr. Chen will be happy to see you both now. Just that way," she said pointing to the open private office door across the office. Atwater and McKnight then walked into Larry's office where he was standing to greet them and shook both their hands. After introductions and pleasantries he motioned for them to sit down in front of his big desk as he walked behind it and sat down.

"My daughter tells me you wish to charter a plane Mr. Atwater," Larry said. "I see from card you are a Vice President with the Hong Kong Shanghai here in town. What is your cargo and where is your destination?"

"Mr. Chen," Atwater said, "I am here with Lieutenant McKnight on confidential bank and British Army business and need your immediate help. I know you visited the Singapore Police this morning about a hijacking of one of your planes to Bombay, and also gave them this gold coin."

Atwater stood and placed a gold sovereign in the middle of Larry's desk and sat back down.

"When informed by the Police they had one of our missing gold coins, I immediately wanted the details and they gave me your name and address." he said. "Let me start from the beginning so you will understand what we're dealing with here. In early 1942, right here in Singapore and just days before the surrender of Singapore, a gold shipment went missing from our vaults. Technically, it belonged to the British Army, but under the care, custody and control of the Hong Kong and Shanghai Bank. After the war, a complete investigation and search was conducted for the gold, and the circumstances of its disappearance, but unfortunately, everyone involved was either killed in the war, or now has amnesia about the matter. We even interrogated all the Japanese officers involved with seizing Singapore and they have no official or unofficial documents or recollections indicating that they confiscated the gold. Needless to say Mr. Chen, we had to reimburse the British Army for the missing gold and it has all been hush-hush since 1946, until today. If you look closely at that coin you will see the 'hka' mint mark which clearly shows it's our gold. Those coins were

minted in 1938 in Hong Kong and the 'a' denotes for the Army.
"

Larry picked up the coin and squinted and saw the mint mark, nodded to Atwater and McKnight and placed the coin back in the center of his desk.

"Mr. Chen, the bank wants its gold back. Somehow a band of adventurers found our buried gold in Malaysia and you folks helped them transport the gold to India, where it will be melted up into trinkets if we don't act fast. I have been instructed by our main headquarters in Hong Kong to immediately put a recovery plan into effect in cooperation with the Army. We've mobilized a special unit of British Commandos under the direction of Lt. McKnight here to help us recover the gold for King and Country. We need to charter the same plane and crew and have them take us to India tomorrow morning. No expense will be spared. I have a cashier's cheque made out to you personally for £7000 to start this project. Whatever final expenses you have just let me know. Won't you help Mr. Chen," he asked placing the cheque beside the gold coin. Larry looked at the cheque for a few moments and reached over and picked it up.

"Nothing would give me greater pleasure than to help you officials recover that gold," he said grinning while picking up the cheque examining it closely.

"Excellent Mr. Chen," Atwater said reaching into his coat pocket and pulling out a manila envelope and placing it on Larry's desk. "Here are the flight details, cargo manifest and destination, which will be Poona, India. I would like to leave for India as early tomorrow morning as possible. Now I would also like to take you and your pilots to dinner tonight at Raffles, say 7 pm. to go over all the details. Can you please meet me in the Long Bar at that time for a cocktail?"

"Unfortunately Mr. Atwater, I have a previous engagement, but would like to suggest my daughter Jasmine take my place. She is number two around here in charge of operations and will completely inform me on your discussions. You can trust her completely. I will arrange the crew to meet you there at 7 pm."

"That is also excellent Mr. Chen," Atwater replied, "I look forward to seeing everyone this evening. And Mr. Chen, the Army will be here tomorrow morning at 6 am to load some special equipment. Will you have ground crew available at that time?

"Of course, already arranged as we speak," Larry said. "The plane will be fueled and ready to depart at 7 am.

"Well then, we'll say goodbye," he said as he and Lt. McKnight stood and shook Larry's hand again. "Oh, I'll need that coin back Mr. Chen. Bank property you know."

Larry picked up the gold coin from his desk and handed it to Atwater, who, along with Lieutenant McKnight, turned for the door and left the office. Atwater walked up to Jasmine's desk and said a personal goodbye telling her he will see her later. Both men then walked out to a waiting black limousine where they climbed in and drove off. Jasmine walked into her fathers' office.

"What was that all about father?" she asked.

"Oh, Mr. Atwater just chartered the '*Lucky Seven*' for a return flight to India tomorrow. Here are the flight details," he said handing the manila envelope to her. "Please prepare the flight plan and make sure the '*Lucky Seven*' is fueled and ready for a 7 am take off. He wanted Cat, Miss Matthews and me to have dinner with him tonight to go over the flight details, but you know I have another most pressing appointment tonight in Johore, so I suggested you might want to attend in my place."

When she heard that the biggest smile ever appeared on her face and she rushed up to her father and gave him a kiss on the cheek already thinking about what she was going to wear for Cat.

"Jasmine, get in touch with Cat and Miss Mathews and tell them they have a charter tomorrow leaving at 7 am and dinner meeting tonight with Mr. Miles Atwater of the Hong Kong Shanghai Bank to discuss the charter. Raffles hotel, Long Bar at 7 pm.," he said smiling at Jasmine not letting on he knows just about everything going on in her heart. "And put everything on my account."

Chapter **19**

Sargent Wong walked into Inspector Barton Musk's office late Tuesday afternoon, observing him reading the afternoon Singapore *Straits Times* newspaper and sipping on his ever present cup of tea.

"Excuse me Inspector," he said, "may I have a word on this 'Oil Exploration' business from this morning?"

"Indeed, indeed," the inspector replied barely looking up from his newspaper and speaking in a rather put offish tone, "enlighten me Sargent."

"First news is there is no company named Malaysian Oil Exploration Co. Ltd. registered in Singapore or Malaysia," Wong recanted as Musk slowly raised his head, "Second we have nothing in our files on that John Jefferies, nor does the Australian Embassy have any record of any passport issued in that name; and third, and this is the really interesting part, that gold coin is pretty rare. The coin book I found says this baby was specially minted in 1938 by the Hong Kong Shanghai Bank, under the supervision of the Bank of England for the British Army. The mint marks 'hka' clearly tell the story. Very few have ever been found in circularization, such that they are worth four or five times face value to a collector."

Sargent Wong then flipped the coin into the air toward Inspector Musk who raised his hand and grabbed it in his fist. Now the story was getting curious.

"Thanks Sargent, good job," Musk replied placing the coin down on his desk, folding his newspaper and setting it aside, and grabbing for the folder with his notes. He was now trying to sort this out in his mind and knew he couldn't just let this go with so many unanswered questions. Realizing he needed help in his investigation, Musk picked up his fountain pen, grabbed a cable gram form and began writing out a message to Scotland Yard in London on the whole affair, specifically asking for any and all information about the gold coin. He checked the box 'routine' traffic which would be transmitted overnight. When he finished the detailed cable he called for Wong who came in and took it to the communications office on the third floor and placed it in the 'in' basket. Within an hour the teletype operator had typed up the message on ticker tape for bulk transmission later that evening. 'SENT' was stamped on the cable form and it was filed away in the days' traffic.

Chapter **20**

Cat and Trish were seated at a table in the Raffles Long Bar ten minutes before seven Tuesday evening enjoying a cocktail, cigarette and listening to the piano man getting them in the mood. This was a first for Cat, meeting with a client for dinner to discuss an air charter and a banker at that! Normally, he just got to the airport and they told him where he was going just before the flight. Thanks to Jasmine's mid afternoon call both he and Trish had time to get ready. Cat was wearing his only light charcoal grey suit and Trish appeared in the Rover with a blue pin striped business type dress and coat combo over a white, low cut blouse and pearls. Cat was getting almost immune to what she wore and how she looked. Well not really, as he was beginning to enjoy all the attention she gathered just by being around. He was thinking of Jasmine just as he spotted her walking towards their table. Many heads were turning in the Long Bar as she approached the table. Cat stood up with a warm smile on his face and looked her in the eyes. She stood at the table even more stunningly dressed than at Larson's going away party the previous Friday night wearing an emerald green, long silk dress with a slit up one side. Cat helped her get seated and sat down himself. Now Cat was surrounded by beauty beyond belief. Overwhelmed is the word that shot through his mind.

"Jasmine you look wonderful this evening," Cat said very properly. With looks around the table all three burst into laughter at his little charade. While Cat ordered another round of drinks, a tall man in a blue suit approached the table.

"Miss Chen," Miles Atwater said, "so nice to see you again. And these are my pilots?"

Cat stood up, shook hands and introduced himself and then pointed to Trish and introduced her. Atwater sat down at the table, motioned the waiter to come over, ordered a drink and surveyed the two extremely attractive women he was seated with. However, he could not stop looking at Trish.

"British Miss Mathews? Leeds?" he asked Trish.

"Yes, my Aussie friend," she boldly replied and then sipped her drink smiling.

"Excellent," he replied with a grin, "You have correctly guessed the Australian sitting with you. Sydney to be exact."

He turned to Cat.

"And our American Captain McCoy, did Larry Chen explain our mission and departure time tomorrow?

"I have been informed of our destination and 7 am departure tomorrow morning for India again, but that's about all I know. I believe Jasmine prepared the flight plan today to be sure we have all the details for a safe flight, as safety is most important to me and my crew."

"That's good to hear, and I can assure you and Miss Mathews will be completely safe on this mission. The Army Commandos will make sure of that," Atwater said looking at them both.

Cat stopped smiling and looked at Atwater in somewhat of disbelief as it appears a few details had been left off in the translation of this charter from father to daughter to Cat.

"I was going to tell everything Cat," Jasmine piped in, "but I haven't had the chance."

"That's fine Jasmine, but perhaps Mr. Atwater would start from the beginning and explain exactly what we're doing," Cat said.

"Of course," Atwater said casually, "Our bank wants the gold back you delivered to India Sunday. The Army commandos are coming along to be sure we get it. Simple as that! You were caught up in a gigantic ruse or hoax over the weekend to move 1000 lbs of gold to India where it will surely be sold and disappear unless we stop them. We're all going back to get it from those smugglers for King and Country. A rather patriotic quest I say. Glad you folks are in."

Cat and Trish looked at each other skeptically and then both looked quizzically at Jasmine who realized her father omitted some details of this charter in explaining it to her. Complete silence occurred at the table while all glanced around at each other and then all eyes finally focused back at Cat.

"Well Captain McCoy," Atwell said, "Are you and Miss Mathews in to recover the Army's gold?

Cat continued to think about this charter and fully confirmed in his mind he had been fooled by Jefferies into thinking they were going to rescue that injured geologist when the practice mission was where they picked up the gold and that's all they wanted. 'Ok Cat,' he said to himself, 'perhaps we can make this right', but it was clearly another of Larry's half baked schemes for maximum monetary reward. He felt everyone staring at him and again he put a faint smile on his face.

"Do we have a choice?" Cat said looking at Atwater.

"Not really," he replied, "your boss cut the deal."

"In that case we're in," Cat said raising his glass to Atwater. Trish raised hers and so did Jasmine. He knew another piece of this adventure was about to begin as the glasses clinked with smiles on everyone's faces.

"Jolly good," Atwater continued, "the Army boys will be at your plane at 6 am to load equipment and then we're off. Once the commandos recover the gold, we'll fly to Hong Kong to put it back in our vaults. You'll probably each get a medal from the King after this mission."

The waiter came over and said that their table was ready in the main dining room where tonight they had a dance band performing. Atwater was first to jump up and escort Trish from her seat. She folded her arm around his and headed to the Good Fortune Dining Room. Cat helped Jasmine up and they strode arm in arm behind Atwater and Trish. When all were seated at their table, Atwater ordered champagne. He had complete command of the menu and suggested what each would like for dinner and he got it right for everyone. The band started playing several songs, dinner was served and the champagne was enjoyed by all. After dinner drinks soon appeared making everything even more lively and friendly. They all got to know each other very well. Atwater went into detail about when the gold was lost in 1942 and was amazed that a single gold sovereign was given to the Singapore police, who in turn called him at the bank asking about its origin. He asked who turned it in, and Cat acknowledged it was him. This started Cat going over the entire sequence of events from practice mission to his crew landing bewildered in Bombay. Atwater kept his eyes on Trish the whole time Cat was talking not really paying much attention to his tale. At the right moment he asked Trish how she had become a pilot. She recanted her story to everyone's delight. Cat knew she had balanced her brains and beauty thing to perfection and was playing Miles Atwater pretty hard. He confirmed in his mind that she was the perfect replacement for Larson Durant. When Atwater asked Trish to dance, Cat jumped at the chance to dance with Jasmine as well. Both couples headed to the dance floor. Maybe the champagne went to his head. Whatever it was, he felt good and with his love with him life was good…really good! And Jasmine was enjoying being with Cat more than words can express. The band played Stardust and he finally had a slow dance he could hold Jasmine tightly against him.

"I am so glad for tonight Jasmine; we're finally together and able to enjoy ourselves. I do love you," he said softly into her ear as they swirled slowly on the dance floor, oblivious to all around them on the crowded floor. Jasmine squeezed him back and was in pure blissful peace in Cat's arms. The music stopped, but they did not stop dancing until Trish tapped Cat on the shoulder.

"Wake up you two. It's late and time to say goodnight," Trish said to Cat and Jasmine, "Mr. Atwell has kindly offered to take me back to the apartment. Perhaps you could take Jasmine home so she won't have to call a taxi."

"Trish, what would I do with out you," he said, "of course I will take Jasmine home."

They all looked at each other and burst out in laughter again at Cat's deadpan, matter of fact statement. The two couples said good night and walked to the lobby of the hotel together in extremely good spirits. In a minute, Atwater's limousine appeared in the curved driveway. The Raffles doormen opened the doors for all to leave. The limousine driver had the door open for Trish and Atwell as they approached. Trish turned and waved at Cat and Jasmine as she got in. Soon they were gone.

Cat walked to the parking area and opened the door of his trusty rusty green Rover for Jasmine.

"I am sorry I don't have a limousine for you to get into, even though you deserve one," he said as he helped her into his Land Rover. As he got in and barely put the key in the ignition, Jasmine moved over and began kissing him. Cat responded by holding her close and adding a few moves of his own. Soon their embrace ended and Jasmine re-seated herself leaning against her big Cat. The Rover started and he began the journey to take her home from their first date, well second date, but their first formal date. They bantered back and forth trying to figure out how this was all going to work knowing without her father's approval they could never be together. Arriving at the well maintained Chen house with its long driveway, Cat turned off the Rover and escorted Jasmine to the door holding her hand. She said goodnight and looked around to be sure no one was looking and kissed Cat again then slid inside. Cat fired up the Rover and returned to 963 Upper Changi Road a very happy man!

Chapter **21**

The Army Commandos arrived early Wednesday and were waiting in their vehicles at the locked gate when Lling Munai arrived on his bicycle just before 6 am. Larry Chen instructed him yesterday to help the Army load their gear and be ready for a 7 am take off. He hurriedly unlocked and opened the gate and pointed to the 'Lucky Seven' sitting serenely on the tarmac near the hanger as the sun was just peaking over the horizon. The two military jeeps and single five ton lorry then roared past him creating a cloud of dust he wanted out of in a hurry. He jumped on his bicycle and pumped as hard as he could to reach the 'Lucky Seven' just as the four Commandos were getting out of their vehicles.

"Say mate," Lieutenant McKnight said to Lling as he set the bikes kickstand quite out of breath, "we've got fourteen drums of aviation petrol and these two jeeps to get aboard this plane pronto. Can you assist?"

"Yes Sir. I am Lling Munai, flight engineer and cargo master of 'Lucky Seven'." Lling replied, "We don't have vehicle ramp, but can get one later."

"Not to worry. Lling, is it?" the Lieutenant snapped back smiling and cock sure of himself, "ramps are in the lorry."

Lling turned and trotted to the 'Lucky Seven', climbed the ladder and opened the cargo man door, climbed inside and then opened the main cargo door full open. He looked out as the lorry backed up to the door where he saw the drums of gasoline, the ramps and other gear waiting to be loaded. In an instant, all four of the Commandos, including the lorry driver, were wheeling the drums onto the plane. They asked Lling where to put them and he pointed to the front and told as far forward as possible. As each drum was loaded he lined them up straddling the centerline left and right. The lorry pulled away when all were on board. He wrestled with the heavy rope blanket over the drums that held them secure down taut to the floor. He finished just as the Commandos had the portable ramps assembled to load the jeeps. Now he was directing traffic inside the 'Lucky Seven' motioning the driver to center his jeep in the cargo bay and move forward until he was just touching the drums. An instant later the second jeep was on board and lined up snug against the first. Lling used cargo chains to secure the jeeps to the floor. The Commandos broke down the ramps and stowed them left and right of the jeeps, along with their other gear. The Lieutenant watched Lling secure the ramps and check everything once more. The time was 6:30 am when the Lieutenant deplaned and called his Commando squad to attention next to the plane, along with the truck driver. After talking to them for a while he shouted 'at ease,' and the men stood with feet apart, arms crossed behind them. He talked directly to the truck driver, who immediately climbed up into the cab of his lorry, started his engine and drove away. Lling observed the Army men's goings on standing in the cargo doorway, when he noticed Cat's Land Rover pull up next to the hangar followed by Larry Chen's car. Cat and Trish got out and both stared at the *'Lucky Seven'* and the Commandos. Larry Chen joined them and exchanged good morning pleasantries. Cat then waved for Lling who came down the ladder and fast walked across the tarmac to meet them.

"Lling, I see our friends are here," Cat said, "and what about their cargo. When will it arrive or was it in that truck we passed on the way in?"

"Cargo loaded Cat from that lorry," Lling responded, "We ready to go. Here is manifest."

Lling handed him the clipboard and Cat looked in cool disbelief at the listing....fourteen drums of aviation gas, two jeeps, ramps and four Commandos with gear. He handed the clipboard to Trish.

"You all know the drill," he said to Trish and Lling, "Lling check the weather up through Rangoon and over to Bombay, get our taxi clearance, and be sure the *'Lucky Seven'* is ready to go including our food and drinks!" Lling took off and turning to Trish he continued, "Let's you and I go inside and review the flight plan, but first please rustle up some coffee for us. Now I need a moment with Larry."

Trish went into the hangar and pilots ready room leaving Cat and Larry alone.

"Larry," Cat said, "I hope they paid you a sack of money for this flight and if it hadn't been the Hong Kong and Shanghai Bank and Army involved with this I would have said no. Are you sure about this deal?"

"Cat, I assure you this will be safe mission," Larry replied, "and yes the Bank paid a huge premium to charter the plane which we need for overhauls. You'll be paid a big bonus when this is over. I even called the Bank and talked with Mr. Atwater's secretary who said he was out of town for a few days. Piece of cake mission for the best pilot in Singapore, if you ask me. Jasmine told me about dinner last night. Sounds like you all had good time with our new Banker friend."

"We had a great time last night and learned a great deal of what's going on here. Atwater's knowledge of the 1942 gold disappearance is amazing. I am not so sure he can pull this gold recovery mission off, but I have to hand it to him for wanting to try. He says we'll be on the ground overnight and will leave for Hong Kong tomorrow afternoon. My concern is disappearing from the Indian air traffic control network if we don't land in Bombay. This shouldn't be a problem as we'll make up a diversionary excuse on our way. Anyway Larry, we'll know the truth when we return in a couple of days after dropping off Atwater and the gold in Hong Kong," he said, "And he says we might even get a medal from the King if this works!"

"That would be great honor Cat. Some of that gold would be better reward! Now please excuse me as I have some paperwork for Atwater to sign when he gets here," Larry said.

After shaking hands, they walked into the hangar where Cat made a bee line for the pilot's ready room as Larry continued on into the office. Cat took his usual chair at the center table and looked at the flight plans Jasmine had prepared yesterday. Sure enough, gas, jeeps and passengers were in the flight orders with destination listed as Poona, India. A map was enclosed showing the abandoned World War II US Army air base in detail far to the east of the small Poona municipal airport, along with some photos the back of which were stamped British Army Intelligence. This was clearly the place he saw Jefferies parachute land on Sunday. Trish returned from the pantry with two cups of hot joe handing one to Cat who immediately sipped the steaming brew.

"Good Lord," he said, "what have we gotten ourselves into? Destination here says Poona, India where we were before, but this time we land at that abandoned airfield. Says we have 5000 ft, paved, but it sure looks narrow and from what I saw last Sunday circling it was pretty overgrown. And I haven't flown that much gas since flying over the 'hump' in 1944. Guess we ask Atwater about this crazy plan when he gets here."

"You require my assistance," Atwater said strolling into the pilots ready room dressed in an Army uniform that matched the Commandos, complete with beret and revolver strapped to his side. Cat and Trish looked up in disbelief at what they were seeing. Banker turned Commando! He walked smiling up to Trish, grabbed her left hand gently lifting it up to his lips and gave it a kiss, "and good morning Miss Trish. I hope you slept well."

"Flattery will still not get what you want Mr. Atwell," Trish said smiling, "but please don't stop trying."

Everyone chuckled at her witty remark. Cat sat back in his chair and looked at the two of them grinning whimsically at each other.

"Look Atwater," Cat blurted out, "Sorry to interrupt you two, but what about landing at that abandoned airfield. Why not land at the municipal airport on the other side of Poona?

"Captain McCoy," he said letting go of Trish's hand while turning to face him, "there are several reasons we must use this airfield. First we don't want to be detected by the Indian authorities, and second it's where you dropped the gold. There will be fresh clues on the ground for us to follow those crooks. After we land the Commandos will cover the plane with camouflage and off load the petrol for your flight engineer to

116

refuel the plane while we're gone. We should have more than enough to reach Rangoon and then fly on to Hong Kong. The entire recovery mission will take less than 24 hours."

"Do you know the real condition of the field?" Cat asked pointedly, "I would hate to crash land and spoil your mission before it starts."

"Army intelligence from our man on the ground yesterday says the airfield is landable. Should be a piece of cake for you Captain McCoy," Atwater said slowly turning and walking away to the office door. "I'll brief you further on the plane about all the mission's details. Now where's Larry Chen? He left me some contracts to sign in his office."

Cat hated that 'piece of cake' phrase beyond belief and wondered why Atwater used it. He was also beginning to think something was not quite right with this whole deal, but again couldn't put his finger on it. And now it appeared Trish was smitten with Atwater, a new development with unknown consequences for him.

"Trish, please do your pre-flight on the 'Lucky Seven'. I'll meet you onboard shortly." He said gathering up all the flight plan papers as she left the pilots office and headed to the 'Lucky Seven'. Cat finished his coffee, stood and reached for his flight map and C-46 manual case. He opened it and checked to be sure his 38 revolver was there with his ammo. Smiling he closed the case and followed Trish to the 'Lucky Seven' after gulping down the rest of his coffee.

Chapter **22**

Cat sat at the end of the Changi airport runway again precisely at 7:15 am running the mighty Pratt and Whitney engines of the '*Lucky Seven*' up and down, conversing with Trish about the preflight checklist and panel dial readings while waiting for final tower permission to take off. He told Trish it was her turn to take off. She smiled, winked and began giving Cat instructions on what to do.

"MalSing 7 you are clear for takeoff," the Changi tower controller announced in their earphones.

"Roger tower," she said after switching to the airport frequency.

Trish pushed the throttles forward to full rpm's, released the brakes and the '*Lucky Seven*' launched down the runway and lifted straight away into another clear February morning and headed north for refueling at Rangoon. Within an hour they reached 15,000 ft and had their airspeed at 225 mph. All post takeoff checklists were complete when she engaged the automatic pilot and pulled her hands free from the yoke and looked over to Cat.

"Well done Trish," he said into the interphone while giving her a thumb's up.

Trish acknowledged the compliment and gave him thumbs up too!

"I think I'll go back and check on our passengers," she said to Cat on the interphone.

He winked at her as she unbuckled and headed back past Lling in his navigator seat to the cargo bay. She surveyed the situation and saw Miles Atwater sitting in the first Jeep on the right side looking at a map of the abandoned airfield and surrounding area. Lieutenant McKnight was sitting is the second jeep cleaning his pistol. The other three Commandos were sitting in the C-46's jump seats inspecting and cleaning their weapons. Trish climbed into the driver's seat next to Miles Atwater.

"And how did my Aussie friend sleep last night," Trish asked as Atwater looked over at her with a smile.

"Splendidly Miss Mathews, except for the short duration, no thanks to you," he said back to her. "Hopefully we can get together again sometime. Say, how about tonight in exotic India?"

"I like your vivid imagination Mr. Atwater," she replied smiling, "but I have a previous engagement." Changing the subject and looking at the map with him she said, "Do you really think we can bring this C-46 into that field and turn her around?"

"Again you and Captain McCoy will have no problems," he said reaching into his pocket for a pack of cigarettes, popping one up for her. "I'll brief you all fully later, after refueling at Rangoon. Care for a smoke?"

"I don't think that's a good idea with all that gas in front of us," she said.

"I love these C-46 figure eight double bubble babies. Finest aircraft design of its time. Did you know this plane was designed for full pressurization and the prototype could go up to 25,000 ft. At our cruising altitude and with the built in air circularization system that changes the air in here every 2 minutes I don't foresee a problem. Do you?"

"Very impressive Mr. Atwater. Your knowledge of the C-46 rivals mine. I guess the smoking lamp is lit," she said with a smile as she slowly pulled the smoke from the pack. He pulled a Zippo lighter from his pocket with a faded and scratched Australian flag painted on the lid and lit her cigarette and then his.

"Interesting lighter you have. May I see it closer? Looks like an antique. Where did you get it?" she said as Atwater handed it to her.

"Oh, got it in a pawn shop I forget where years ago. It's engraved with the name Lt. Kincaid. I keep it as a good luck piece," he said as Trish read the name.

"Works like a charm," she said wryly flicking the lid open and closed before handing it back, "has it made you lucky yet?"

"I'd have to say yes. There are echoes from the past you can hear if you hold it just so next to your ear," he said holding it to his right ear. "Yes, I'm getting something now. Our Lieutenant Kincaid has just told me he approves of you from across time."

Trish blushed for the first time she could remember as she looked back at Atwater and found it difficult to believe he had found the key to re-awakening emotions long hidden and suppressed inside her. This one just popped to the surface and felt exhilarating. Then just as fast she wanted her control back and pushed the blush back down inside, resuming her perky and witty persona and wondering what he would trigger next.

"Thank you Miles. I see you have been working on your flattery thing since this morning. What will you come up with this afternoon," she said trying to find a way to change the subject again.

"Now I see your troops are getting ready for action back there. Are you expecting difficulties?"

"Trish we're ready for anything. Being prepared is the key. Knowing your adversary, the terrain and obstacles that must be overcome are what these men have been trained for. They are the best. They overlook nothing and always have a second plan in case the first goes bad.

"How come you sound more like a soldier than a banker," she asked.

"Simple, I used to be a soldier in the war and flew in DC-3's pushing cargo out over New Guinea and Borneo and all the islands in between during the War for the Australian Air Force. The banker appeared after the war. Now you know everything," he said with a grin.

Trish laughed and continued smiling at Atwater when Cat walked up to the jeep.

"Mind taking over up front while I visit the loo in the back," he said walking past them.

"Sure boss," she replied as she looked at Atwater and then got out of the jeep and went back to the cockpit where Lling was sitting in her seat minding the controls.

"Ok Lling. I'm back," she said as Lling got out of her seat and retook his navigator radioman position.

The 'Lucky Seven' arrived at Rangoon just after twelve noon, landed and refueled as fast as they could. Lling inspected the engines and made sure the oil tanks were topped off as well. Cat, Trish, Miles Atwater and the Commandos all got out of the plane during the refueling to stretch their legs and tend to personal business. Cat filed his India flight plan at the office, which would teletype it to Bombay with their estimated time of arrival. Within 30 minutes all were back on board and the cargo man door was shut. Trish hot started the starboard engine, which coughed and came to life easily and the port engine soon followed. Once again they were taxing for takeoff for the last six hour leg of their journey to Poona, India. Minutes later the 'Lucky Seven' was climbing to cruising altitude heading west over the Bay of Bengal. They would break the coast of India in four hours which again mandated a flight confirmation clearance with the Indian Air Control authorities.

Chapter **23**

"Hyderabad, this is MalSing7, Singapore charter to Bombay checking in for flight control over," Cat spoke into the microphone as they passed into the Indian subcontinent.

"Hyderabad control here. MalSing7 approved for Bombay eta 1800. Weather cloudy and chance of rain on arrival," the Indian controller spoke in excellent English.

"So glad that's over Trish. Now only our mechanical breakdown radio call to Bombay to say we're returning to Hyderabad and we're home free for 24 hours anyway," as Cat spoke to her on the interphone. "Two hours to landing. I think I'll go back and talk with Atwater and Lt. McKnight about the landing. Keep us straight on for Poona and bring us up to 235 knots. I want to be sure we land before dark."

Cat unbuckled his seatbelt and walked back to Miles Atwater who was sitting and talking with Lieutenant McKnight in the second jeep.

"I think its time you gentlemen told me your plan. We're less than two hours to landing on that air strip and it will be close to dark. One shot is all we got and then we must proceed to Bombay," Cat pronounced.

"I fully understood Captain McCoy. Do your best which is all we can ask. As you've said before safety is first," Atwater replied fully baiting Cat to make the risky landing by agreeing with him fully. "If you do get us in, Lt. McKnight's Commandos will take over from there. After we cover the plane in camouflage and get the fuel and jeeps off, we'll take you and Miss Mathews with us to a former religious retreat villa near where we're going. It's practically a resort with all the tropical comforts of home. We'll spend the night there, while our Indian born Commando, Corporal Desai over there, reconnoiters the area for our gold smugglers. He is very familiar with that area and hand picked for this mission. A report from our ground informant says they are still in the area. Corporal Desai will ferret them out and then we will retrieve our gold in the morning simple as that!"

"What about Lling our flight engineer? Cat asked.

"He'll stay with the plane tonight to guard it and get it refueled using the electric fueling pump we brought along. When you signal him tomorrow from the jeep with the walkie talkie we're leaving with him, he'll get the plane ready for a fast departure." McKnight said.

"Seems you two have thought of everything except the local authorities," Cat retorted, "think they will just let you waltz into town with guns blazing?"

"Captain McCoy, we're landing in the middle of nowhere and will go as quietly and peacefully to and from the town of Wagholi as possible. And as you've pointed out in the dark this evening. Worry not Captain as everything is under control." Atwater replied.

Cat continued to look at Atwater and McKnight wondering where their cool calmness was coming from as parts of his body were beginning to pucker up. He told both of them to be ready for the landing and said Lling would give them a ten minute warning to touchdown. Atwater said he wanted to be in the cockpit with them in the jump seat as advisor and Cat agreed. He then returned to the cockpit and retook his seat and put his headphones on.

"Trish and Lling listen up. Here's the plan," he said into the interphone, "If we can land, you Lling will stay with the plane overnight and refuel her tomorrow morning and be ready for a fast departure in the early afternoon. Trish, you and I are guests of the Army tonight at some villa they have arranged accommodations. Lling, I will make this up to you when we get back."

"I scared of tigers," Lling replied rather nervously and pale looking as Cat glanced back at him.

"Not to worry, I'll leave you my trusty 38 that's in the manual case to scare the tigers away," he said trying to calm Lling down as he pointed to the case behind his seat. Lling nodded and appeared to calm down.

"Miss Matthews, any tiger problems or phobias with you?" he said comically.

"Piece of cake," she said smiling knowing Cat hated those three words with a passion and the dirty look he gave her back confirmed it.

"Trish, we're gonna float and drop the 'Lucky Seven' like a bumble bee onto that old fighter strip. Full flaps and hard down as close to the end of that runway as I can get it. We then battle our way to the end with the jungle scrub and small trees growing right against the pavement left and right. The pictures show the height of that scrub to be 8 to 10 feet tall which means we'll be slicing the top two feet all the way to the end for a turn around. On the ground we'll decide how and where to turn this beast around. I think the metal leading wing edges will withstand the beating, but not sure. When I touch down, I want you to kill the throttles and feather the props. I'll keep her steady and brake hard, but won't let her skid. You be ready if I need help. Last thing we need is to change a tire out here. We'll dodge any close trees if we can. If we can't see the pavement when we get there I told Atwater we go to Bombay and he agreed."

"The wing tips will clear most of the bush and just bend it," Trish said "No damage to the '*Lucky Seven*' is what I see."

"Glad you are confident about this Trish. We'll know for sure in a little more than an hour," Cat replied. "Now, I better call Bombay and tell them we're returning the Hyderabad."

Cat made the radio call to Bombay and then broke out the maps and pictures of the abandoned US Army airfield again for all to see. Cat liked the fact the runway was east to west, which meant what setting sunlight there was should be bouncing off the pavement into their eyes. The crew tried to relax, but kept on edge because of the landing risks. After an hour they were rapidly approaching Poona. Cat told Lling to tell the passengers we were about to land. When he came back Atwater followed him and took the jump seat that folded out into the isle between Cat and Trish.

"Look for the lake and line up on the left of it due west," Atwater shouted out for Cat and Trish to hear. Within five minutes the lake came into view and they steered to the left. It shimmered in the setting sun.

"There's the runway ahead," Trish spoke into the interphone as simultaneously she and Cat held up their free hand with fingers crossed. Atwater smiled at the whimsical gesture.

"Roger," Cat said laughing as he found the field in the horizon reflecting the setting sun off the pavement. It was a clear crimson beacon pulling the '*Lucky Seven*' down. Trish applied full flaps as they descended with Cat nudging the throttles forward to keep up the airspeed. They were floating down fast just above stall as Cat set the '*Lucky Seven*' down hard as they crossed the end of the runway. The C-46 bounced once and settled down with Cat applying full brakes while Trish cut the throttles and feathered the props. They were slicing some of the vegetation left and right, but Trish was right, most of it was pushed under the wingtips. As they taxied and approached the end of the runway Cat pulled off the right side of the runway into the bush, locked the left brake and spun the '*Lucky Seven*' around and pointed her right down the runway again for an easy take off. Trish cut the ignition switches and the engines slowly came to a stop.

"Amazing job you two," Atwater said unbuckling and standing up. "You two certainly know your stuff."

"Well save your thanks until we take off tomorrow," he replied. "Now Trish and I must inspect the plane for damage, which you're gonna pay for!"

Lling already had the cargo door open and ladder extended when Cat, Trish, Atwater and the Commandos climbed down to the runway to survey the situation. While Cat and Trish began walking the plane's perimeter, the Commandos climbed back into the plane and started assembling the ramps. Lling was busy uncovering the gas drums and untying the jeeps hold down chains. One of the Commandos started the second jeep and slowly backed it out down the ramp after some maneuvering.

Then he walked up the ramp and backed the first jeep out. Next for off loading came the fourteen aviation gas drums. They were manhandled to the cargo door and each rolled down one ramp very carefully with two commandos working each drum with two standing in the cargo bay holding taut a rope tether. By the time Trish and Cat had fully inspected the plane, the cargo bay was empty. They reported to Atwater that the leading wing edges had a few dents inflicted that needed minor repair, but the 'Lucky Seven' was ship shape. As they were standing talking next to the jeeps, the Commandos covered the plane with camouflage nets as the sun was nearly set. After completing that task, they unloaded the gas pumping apparatus and hoses and were showing Lling how it worked. Next they gave him the walkie talkie and went over its operation, which he already knew. They also gave him several flashlights. With all the food and drink on the plane, he would have a nice quiet evening. Now that everything was done, Cat and Trish were asked to get into the back seat of Atwater's jeep. Lieutenant McKnight was driver. In the other jeep were the three Commando's with Corporal Desai as driver. Trish and Cat waived goodbye to Lling, who held up Cat's 38 pistol above his head waving it back and forth as both jeeps headed for the other end of the runway.

In the dusky darkness, with the runway illuminated by the jeeps headlights, it looked like a private two lane highway fully screened on both sides by the scrub. Turning around a minute later Cat could not see the 'Lucky Seven' at all. Finally the jeeps headlights picked up the scrub wall at the end of the runway.

Both jeeps slowed and then stopped. Corporal Desai got out of his lead jeep and walked from right to left and stopped. He pointed to the scrub in front of him and returned to his jeep and waved for Lt. McKnight in the second jeep to follow.

Approaching slowly, the first jeep drove into the scrub and disappeared. Lt. McKnight followed and Cat could see that a lot of the vegetation had been recently cut and driven over making it easy for them to proceed. All in their jeep shifted to the center to avoid being whip lashed by the rebounding bush. Twenty seconds later they were on a narrow gravel road approaching the stopped first jeep. The bush they drove over stood back up and acted as a hidden garage door to the field. Clearly corporal Desai knew where he was going. They followed the gravel road until they reached a broken metal fenced gate that lead to another road. One of the Commandos jumped out and opened it for both jeeps to pass through and closed it again. They had turned left heading north and with the commando back in the first jeep they proceeded on this extremely bumpy road. After another ten minutes of jostling they reached an intersection and saw a sign pointing to the right for Wagholi 25 km. The lead jeep turned right onto this better paved two lane road and took off. In forty five minutes driving they reached the outskirts of Wagholi. Jeep number one slowed at a narrow road on the right and turned with the second jeep following. They were now on another bumpy road from hell and had to go slow. After a quarter mile, the first jeep stopped at a walled compound entrance where they were going to spend the night. Corporal Desai got out of his jeep, knocked on the eight foot high gates. One side opened and he went into the compound. Both gates were then thrown open and the jeeps drove through and stopped, waiting for Corporal Desai and another man to close the gates. Both then jumped into the back seat of the first jeep and continued into the compound where various buildings appeared left and right in the jeeps headlights. They approached a large building with an electric light burning out front with many people standing on a porch. The first jeep stopped in front. Lt. McKnight pulled along side and turned off his jeep. Everyone got out. The people on the porch, including elderly and young men and women, and children completely surrounded a beaming Corporal Desai as he climbed the porch.

They all began greeting him with palms pressed together, nods and repeating 'namaste.' The men all shook his hand vigorously one by one. Cat observed that all had their finest clothing on, with the women in colorful sari's and the men their kurta pajamas. The atmosphere was celebration like, which he didn't understand. He had only observed this type of reception once while stationed with the Army Air force in Darjeeling in 1945 at a local wedding.

Corporal Desai looked to Miles Atwater and motioned for him to step onto the porch, while the other Commandos continued to stand by their jeep with Lt. McKnight. Again he was greeted with more pressed palms with 'namaste' spoken to him and handshakes. Atwater did the same gesture to each person with a pressed palm greeting and returned each 'namaste' greeting with a nod. Two of the little children, perhaps five or six years old, rushed up to Atwater and grabbed him by each leg hugging him and not wanting to let go. Everyone on the porch laughed as Atwater tried to steady himself. Soon the other Commandos walked up on the porch one by one and were introduced by Corporal Desai to everyone and each received the same greeting. Now only Cat and Trish were standing by their jeep alone observing the goings on.

"Ok you two. Come on up here," Atwater said motioning to Cat and Trish to join him on the porch. "We are in paradise and these are relatives of Corporal Desai and you two are their guests of honor tonight. Won't you say hello?"

Both Cat and Trish were in turn greeted individually by everyone on the porch with wonderful, happy smiles just like everyone else. Cat knew the Indian greeting protocol and did the pressed palm greeting with each person. Trish picked up the proper greeting etiquette and clearly had fun greeting everyone. Cat suffered the same treatment by the children as they clung to his legs not wanting to let go. As he teetered, everyone laughed in his struggle to keep standing.

"You will all be taken to your bungalow to freshen up and get settled. Please all meet around back in the patio area for refreshments and a wonderful meal," Atwater said to the Commandos, Cat and Trish. "There are only candles in the bungalow, but each has running water and I think you all have flashlights just in case."

With that Corporate Desai spoke to the young men and women on the porch in his Indian dialect and they each came up to the Commandos, Cat and Trish and motioned them to follow. Trish was whisked away into the main house after removing her boots by two of the young women. Cat, Atwater and the Commandos were escorted by lantern light by two young men to the nearby bungalow buildings that had two separate rooms in each. Cat was the first to be dropped off with his guide going inside and lighting the candles for him. He thanked the young man with a pressed palm greeting. Atwater was placed in the next room and the commandos were placed in two other bungalows farther down the path.

Cat walked inside his room, closed the door and wondered to himself what was wrong with this entire picture, but couldn't put his finger on anything. He freshened up and tried to figure out what was coming next.

Chapter **24**

As Cat walked back and around to the rear of the main house he saw three Commandos with Atwater sitting at one table having beers and laughing. The patio and lanai was beautiful with five tables set up for dinner. The Indian men, both young and old, were at two tables. The children were running around playing and kicking a ball. The women came in and out of the main house kitchen carrying bowls of food and drink and were serving everyone appetizers and as he got closer recognized as samosas.

"Over here mate," Atwater said as he motioned for Cat to sit down. "How about a cold Kingfisher?"

"Don't mind if I do" Cat responded as Atwater handed him an opened bottle.

"You know Cat; these men have some fascinating stories. They are world travelers and each battle tested. Makes you a little humble to be in their company. I hear you had 'hump' flying duty right here in India during the war. What was that like?"

Before Cat could answer, Corporal Desai walked up in everyday Indian clothing and asked to speak to Atwater and McKnight. They both got up from the table and moved away. After conversing for some time they parted with Corporal Desai going back into the main building with Atwater and McKnight rejoining the table.

"He's going into town to find the bad guys," Atwater said. "Won't be long now!"

Atwater asked Cat again about his 'hump' flying experience and he recanted his story and the fact the flying got easier as the Japanese air force was neutralized at Lassio, Burma. Up until that time you never knew if a rough Jap fighter would be after you if you took a short cut.

"Other than the tedium of flying overweight C-46 aircraft on an exhausting schedule seven days a week over the Himalayas to Kunming, China, it was a piece of cake," Cat said and couldn't believe he let slip these three words he hated.

All at the table continued to talk, joke and laugh until someone appeared coming from the house. All conversation stopped to dead silence as Trish slowly walked toward them and stopped. She had been transformed into an Indian beauty. The dark red sari she wore with its exquisite white and gold embroidery was something to behold. Her hair was combed straight back and tied into a bun. She was also exquisitely made up with a red dot on her forehead. The gold necklace and bracelets she wore accentuated her sari. The Indian women came out of the house and stood to the side as all eyes focused on Trish. She pressed her hands together with a slight smile on her face and slowly nodded toward Miles Atwater. He stood up and walked over to her as everyone looked on and extended his arm. Saying nothing she held his arm as they walked slowly to the table. Cat and the Commandos began clapping their hands. A whistle was heard and then everyone joined in the clapping and cheers. It looked like they were walking down the isle after being married. The uniformed British officer and his Indian beauty.

"Is anyone going to offer a lady a beer," Trish asked beaming as she arrived at the table.

Everyone laughed and made a place for her to sit down. A glass appeared with beer in it. She lifted it looking around the table as everyone else did the same thing. She looked at Miles smiling and took a sip. All eyes were still on her and she loved the attention, especially from Miles with his wry remarks. In several minutes the atmosphere cooled down and everything got back to almost normal, but clearly Trish was the center of attention and attraction for the Commandos, Cat and Atwater. The Indian women then served dinner to everyone and nothing but laughter and high spirits could be felt throughout the meal, where everyone was bantering back and forth. At its conclusion, the Commandos left the table for a smoke leaving Cat, Trish and Atwater behind. Strong tea and desert pastries were served to them.

"Mind telling us a little more about yourself," Cat asked Atwater, "Do you have brothers and sisters?

"Yes, a younger sister and older brother who was killed in the war in Malaysia." Atwater replied.

I'm sorry to hear that," Cat responded.

"Thanks you. He was a Lieutenant in the Australian Artillery defending Tebong Station, Malaysia, when he was ordered to lead a secret mission. On completion of that mission and returning to Singapore his squad was ambushed by a force of Japanese Army scouts who had just entered the battle for
134

Malaysia. They killed everyone in my brother's squad and buried all seven of them in a shallow mass grave beside a road. This all happened in late January 1942. I was still in high school at the time, eventually joined the Australian Air Force and served as a loadmaster on DC-3's over Borneo and New Guinea. Our family heard nothing about my older brother until after the war when in late 1945 we were visited at home by two Army officers. I can remember that day like it was yesterday. One carried a valise and the other an Australian flag. My mother answered the door bell and showed them into the living room expecting the worst. I happened to be home and so was my father. As we gathered together, the Army Captain told us officially that my brother had been killed in action in Malaysia. My mother and father sat before them as they saluted and presented her the flag and several medals on behalf of a grateful nation. Needless to say we all cried, but we knew after all this time the inevitability of his never coming home. My father asked if they had any more information on his death and where Gerald's remains were and the circumstances. That's my brothers name Gerald."

Trish and Cat listened intently and sipped their tea as Atwater continued his story.

"The officer opened his valise and removed an envelope containing a two page letter, addressed to my parents that explained as much as the Army knew. Seems a Japanese officer confessed to ordering the execution of my brother and others in his squad. He was also tried on other war crimes he committed while running the infamous Changi prison camp. He lead the crimes investigators to the spot they were buried. The Army reburied the seven in an official ceremony at the Pasir Panjang Military Cemetery in Singapore. I went to that ceremony along with my parents and met the families of the others killed. It was a very moving experience. I followed the Japanese officers' war crimes trial right up until he was hanged in 1947. The whole affair has raised many unanswered questions to this day as to why he was on that road in the first place. Anyway, my brother was a great person and I miss him everyday."

"A very moving story Miles. I can tell you two were very close," Cat spoke sympathetically.

"Yes, I can see you thought very highly of him," Trish said, "have you gotten any answers to your questions yet?

"Not really. Lot's of Army mumbo jumbo and dead ends. It was a crazy mixed up time at the beginning of the war for those Aussies involved and not very well managed. I guess those answers may never come," Atwater replied.

Corporal Desai came walking up to the table quite out of breath and perspiring and asked to speak to Atwater, who motioned for Lieutenant McKnight to join them. They huddled up away from the table out of listening distance of Cat and Trish. After they spoke McKnight waved for his Commandos to come over. Now all were standing listening to Desai. Whatever was being said the Commandos went from jolly, fun loving folk to poker face in an instant. A minute later the Commandos started walking to their bungalows. Atwater returned to the table and sat down.

"Sorry about the drama. The bad guys are holed up with our gold in a guarded compound across to the east of Wagholi. We're going to move out at 0330 hours and assault them at dawn. You two will stay here until we return, I guess before 8 am and then we dash for your plane. Will you be ready?" Atwater said.

"Can do Atwater. We'll be standing by." Cat said as Trish nodded too.

"Great! I think I will say good night to you good folks. See you in the morning."
136

Atwater stood up, reached over and lifted Trish's right hand and kissed it giving her a wink.

"Marvelous outfit Trish. You are truly something to behold," he said turning and walking away.

For the second time that day Trish blushed, but in the candlelight didn't try to conceal it at all. She just looked at Miles Atwater walking away with a wonderful smile on her face as she looked at Cat who was looking back at her.

"Yes, perhaps we should call it an evening Trish," he said standing at the same time Trish did.

He wished her a good night and headed to his bungalow. Trish turned and walked into the house, where the Indian women were waiting for her. She walked with them to her room on the other side of the main house and slowly took off her sari with their help. They folded it neatly, washed the red dot from her forehead and wished her a good night with pressed palms. She did the same thing and bowed to them until they left her room. She stood there in the candlelight and looked at herself in the mirror. She thought about redoing her hair, but decided to leave it just as it was. Sleep would not come as her mind was racing and thinking of Miles Atwater. She was beginning to think he might have the keys to her stored up emotions after all.

Cat returned to his room suffering from sensory input overload from all the events of the week. He sat in the chair next to the candle beside the table for the longest time wide awake enjoying a cigar. His mind was racing so fast going over the last few days, and then focusing on Jasmine, and then back to everything that has happened since Larson Durant left the previous Friday. Then the next moment he was awakened by the sound of the jeeps leaving the compound. The candle was out, so he switched on his flashlight. 3:30 am it was. He had slept in the chair for over four hours.

Chapter **25**

The teletype machine in the communication office on the third floor of Singapore Police headquarters chattered away at seven Thursday morning with a message that read:

> Attn Inspector Barton Musk, Singapore PD.
> Top Priority One. Intercept and hold all
> involved with gold report. Gold shipment
> lost from vaults of Hong Kong and Shanghai
> Bank just before Singapore surrender in
> 1942. Gold belongs to British Army. Have
> dispatched agent Inspector David
> Hildebrand from Hong Kong to assist in
> investigation. Arrival Singapore 3 pm local
> Thursday on special Army plane. Please
> advise this office interim action taken. /s/
> Dowdy, Chief Inspector, Scotland Yard.

The message finished and was torn off the printer with many others. Since it was a priority one communiqué, it was placed in a special red sealed envelope and hand delivered to Inspector Barton Musk's desk. When he arrived just before 8 am, with cup of tea in hand, he saw the red envelope on his desk, walked over and place his tea down, opened it and read the message. The envelope fell to the floor as he turned and ran over to Sargent Wong's desk with the message and handed it to him. In thirty seconds both men were racing down the stairs to Musk's private patrol car.

Wong drove north to the Changi Airfield as fast as he could with siren blaring and Musk urging him on over and over saying, 'faster man, faster.' They finally raced through the gates of the MalSing Air Charter Service and slammed on the brakes at the front door of the hangar. They hurriedly walked into the offices and were met by Larry Chen and Jasmine who were wondering what the siren was all about.

"Inspector," Larry said as Musk and Wong walked past Jasmine nodding hello and approached him, "what is going on please?"

"Mr. Chen, let's go into your office," Musk said.

"Of course, follow me," Larry said turning around and fast walking himself to his office with Musk and Wong right behind.

"Mr. Chen I need to talk to your pilots again about that story you told me about flying some heavy sacks to India at gunpoint. We've been told by Scotland Yard that gold coins were in those sacks."

"Yes, I know about gold from Commando Lieutenant McKnight and Mr. Miles Atwater of the Hong Kong and Shanghai Bank who chartered the same plane and crew yesterday morning for a return flight to Poona, India," Larry said smiling, "Atwater was very happy you gave him the gold

139

coin and referred me to help get the banks gold back. And with those Army Commandos along, I know they'll get it back for you. Atwater told us we get medal from the King for helping when this is over."

Inspector Musk and Sargent Wong looked at each other in disbelief trying to understand what they were hearing as it made no sense to them.

"Are you saying Mr. Chen, Bank and British Army representatives are now on a mission to recover the gold?" Musk asked.

"Yes. Left 7 am yesterday morning with jeeps and Commandos. All are in India now," Larry exclaimed as he found Atwater's business card and handed it to Musk, "Here is card of Miles Atwater."

Musk took the card, looked at it closely and asked Larry if he could use his phone. He then dialed up Miles Atwater's phone number at the Hong Kong and Shanghai Bank.

"Miles Atwater here, may I help you."

"Yes you can. I am Inspector Barton Musk of the Singapore Police. Did you charter a plane from the MalSing Air Charter Service at Changi field yesterday to take some Army Commandos to India to get your stolen gold back?

"Inspector, I can assure you I don't know what you are talking about. I just got in last night from meetings since last week in Hong Kong. Someone is pulling a joke on you I'm afraid."

"So Mr. Atwater, you know nothing about the Bank's missing gold, an Army Lieutenant named McKnight, or a Mr. Larry Chen over here at the air charter service?"

"Again no to all that. You have me completely mystified," he said in a perplexed tone, "this must be a fantastic joke someone
140

is pulling on you. I can assure you Inspector the Bank is not involved with this matter."

"Yes sir, I see. Someone must be playing a joke on us. Sorry for disturbing you Mr. Atwater. Good day sir," the inspector said as he slowly placed the handset onto the receiver and looked over at Sargent Wong with Larry Chen staring on.

"Atwater says he never heard of our Mr. Chen here, nor the Army Lieutenant, did not charter the plane and knows nothing about the gold."

All three men stared at each other in silence for the longest time.

"Mr. Chen, you say your plane is in Poona, India? He asked.

"Yes. They are there now. We have flight plan, cargo and passenger manifest and maps of abandoned airfield they land at. Do you want to see Inspector? Larry said.

"Yes, I may need to borrow them all for a while if you don't mind," Musk replied as Larry led the Inspector and Sargent Wong to Jasmine's desk where she gave them copies of the flight plan and maps. After looking at the flight documents for a minute, both said goodbye to Larry and Jasmine Chen, walked out to their car and returned to Singapore Police headquarters. Sargent Wong drove just as fast returning, but Musk sat quietly this time trying to put the pieces of this puzzle he faced together.

Arriving back at his office Musk told Wong to get Colonel Edmond Fitzwald over at the Bukit Army Barracks on the phone for him.

"Hello Edmond, Barton Musk here," he said, "How are you doing my friend?

"Barton, so good to hear your voice. I hope this is not about that speeding ticket on the parkway," he replied.

141

"No, No, No. I am calling on official business Ed. Scotland Yard business to be exact. Seems a Lieutenant McKnight and three other Commando from your outfit are on a mission to India to get the Army's gold back. They left yesterday morning by transport from Changi field. Destination is Poona, India. Can you tell me what you've heard from your men?"

"Afraid I don't know what you are talking about Ed. We have no mission to India going on now, and I am looking at a roster here and we have no Lieutenant McKnight anywhere stationed in Singapore. Did you check the Navy boys? Maybe some Royal Marines?"

"No our informant said Army Commandos with jeeps were loaded on the transport," Musk replied. "There is 1000 pounds of the Army's gold at stake here. Say, do you have any contacts with the Indian Air Forces?"

"Yes, Vijay Singh is Commanding General of IAF and personal friend of mine since the war. He's over in Bombay and I can teletype him, or better yet, I can call him on your behalf to see what he can do. Can you come over to the barracks with all the particulars?"

"I am on my way Ed. Thanks and goodbye," he said.

Inspector Musk and Sargent Wong gathered up all the information they had and drove over to the Bukit Barracks with siren blaring and arrived in record time. Colonel Ftizwald greeted them at his office and they walked to the communications room where Musk dictated a top secret message to the teletype operator for immediate transmission to Bombay laying out all the facts and requesting intercept of the MalSing7 C-46 aircraft which landed at Poona. When they were finished and back into Fitzwald's office the Colonel tried to telephone General Singh in Bombay, but could not get an immediate circuit to go through. As they were waiting Musk went through the entire story of what he knew and showed the message from Scotland Yard. After an hour of waiting with no luck in getting a circuit to Bombay, Musk and Wong said goodbye to the Colonel. Musk asked that if he did get through to relay the message again to intercept, hold and detain the plane and all passengers and crew and notify him at Singapore Police Headquarters.

Chapter **26**

Cat and Trish were drinking a chai tea in his bungalow room just before 8 am and talking when they heard the jeeps approaching with horns honking madly. They stepped out of his room and watched the gates flung open with the heavily laden jeeps, driven by Atwater and Lieutenant McKnight, roar past to the main house still honking their horns where they stopped. They ran to the jeeps as Atwater jumped out, as did the four Commandos.

"Rough go back there," Atwater said to Cat and Trish as they approached breathing heavily, "We haven't much time and must get out of here. The bad guys may be following us."

As they were talking the Indian men, women and children came out of the main house. Corporal Desai spoke to them and they all nodded and turned to Atwater smiling and walked up in a semi-circle apparently were saying goodbye to him. He did the pressed palm greeting to each. Next he walked up to Corporal

Desai, shook his hand, said goodbye and gave him a hug. He repeated his personal handshake with Corporal Standish and gave him a hug as Lt. McKnight and Corporal Perth each got into the a jeeps drivers seat.

"Captain Atwater, we have to go," Lt. McKnight said as both jeeps started.

He turned to Trish and asked her to get in the front seat with McKnight. He handed Cat the walkie talkie and told him to reach his man Lling when they got in range and pointed to the jeep with Corporal Perth. Atwater then jumped into the back seat of McKnight's jeep behind Trish, patted McKnight on the shoulder who backed up and then sped toward the gate. Atwater was waving at everyone in front of the house and they all waved back. Perth followed with Cat hanging on. He was trying to sort out what he had just witnessed. Trish looked back at Atwater smiling and noticed he was sitting on a sack with another just beside it. Had they gotten the gold?

They sped and jostled on the bumpy road and finally turned on the paved road toward the abandoned airfield and picked up speed. Cat kept trying to reach Lling on the walkie talkie when finally he heard Lling.

"Captain Cat Lling here."

"Fire up the starboard engine and get ready to take off pronto. We will arrive in 10 minutes."

"Roger Cat," Lling said into his walkie talkie.

Lling pulled the camouflage off the 'Lucky Seven', climbed onboard and raced to the cockpit and began the starboard engine start procedure by hitting the primers, starter and then the ignition. The Pratt and Whitney engine sputtered, coughed and started in the usual cloud of smoke and then settled down. Lling looked out the cockpit window and could see the two

145

jeeps fast approaching from the end of the runway. Shortly they were at the plane, pulled to the cargo door side, stopped and everyone jumped out.

"Trish, get the other engine started as I help with the sacks, Cat said as she ran over to the cargo bay door ladder, climbed up and disappeared.

All four men struggled with the sacks getting them onboard the aircraft and then climbed down the ladder and stood together at the jeeps. Atwater faced the two Commandos.

"Well, this is goodbye for now my friends, "Atwater said as shook hands with McKnight and Perth and gave both of them hugs and pats on the back. "See you soon and thank Desai again for his hospitality."

Trish got the port engine started in a roar and gust of wind as Cat shook hands with them and figured out they were staying behind. Atwater climbed the ladder and helped Cat into the cargo bay. Perth and McKnight stood facing Atwater and both saluted. Atwater returned the salute and then helped Cat close the cargo door. Through the window he could see the jeeps roar off down the runway.

"Mind telling me what that was about," Cat asked walking to the cockpit, "Do you know those men personally?"

"You might say that, but we have to hurry. I expect we're going to be greeted by the Indian Air Force shortly and we need to be gone from here."

Trish had the engines ready for take off when Cat took his seat. Lling was buckled into his navigator seat and Atwater took the jump seat between Cat and Trish.

"Let's go Trish," he said as she pushed the throttles to the stops and took her foot off the brakes. The 'Lucky Seven' launched down the runway gathering speed until Trish pulled gently back on the yoke and she lifted off into the mid morning sun. As they continued east, Cat could see out his window the two jeeps on the road traveling back to Wagholi. They were headed directly for the compound and sure enough, Cat spotted it, and banked the plane so Trish and Atwater could see everyone on the ground waving at them. Trish straightened out the ship and began climbing to 15,000 ft. Atwater put his headphone on and keyed the interphone mike.

"Slight change of plan my fine pilots. I want you to set a new non-stop course for Nha Trang, Vietnam."

Cat and Trish both turned in their seats and looked at a smiling Atwater. They also looked to see if he had a gun pointing at them.

"Are you hijacking us like the boys did earlier this week? Cat asked.

"Heavens no! You see I forget about a very important appointment tonight with a close friend. I've something to drop off with him and then we'll go to Hong Kong. I told him all about you both and he really wants to meet you. Flying empty as we are, with almost full tanks means we have plenty of gas to fly non-stop. Could be a big problem if we stop in Rangoon."

Cat and Trish looked at each other and were beginning to feel déjà vu as the second hijacking in four days was unfolding.

"Do we have a choice?" they both shouted out loud in unison.

"Not really," Atwater replied smiling patting his holster for both to see.

"In that case it's off to Nha Trang. Trish please set a new course for Mr. Atwater and re-calculate our fuel to be sure we can make it safely."

"Roger Cat," Trish replied pulling out new maps and charts. After 15 minutes, she made a course correction and confirmed to Cat that they would have a 400 gallon reserve after the 10 hour, 2400 mile flight, well within the safety margin.

"Oh, something else flight crew," Atwater informed them, "When we are well past Hyderabad approaching the coast, I want you to check in with them and say you had to land in Poona for emergency repairs. Also say your radio burned out in an electrical fire and has been temporarily fixed, but for how long you don't know. Then announce your destination as Nha Trang, Vietnam, ETA 19:00 hours local. Please don't tell them your location. When they demand to know, say your radio is fading out again and is overheating. Say you'll call them right back and click. Silence."

Cat and Trish looked at each other again and then to Atwater.

"Do we have a choice?" they both shouted out again in unison smiling.

"Not really," Atwater replied patting his holster.

Cat made the radio call to Hyderabad control and it went exactly as Atwater had scripted. He learned they had an all points bulletin out as to their whereabouts and requested they promptly land in Hyderabad. Atwater listened and chuckled, but Cat and Trish did not think it amusing. They passed the coast and were headed across the Bay of Bengal on a beeline to Bangkok, Thailand when the two Indian Air Force Typhoon fighters appeared on both sides of the plane.

"Oh boy Atwater. We have company left and right. Now what?" he said on the interphone.

"See what they want and remind them you are having radio problems. Tell them your flight plan is non-stop to Nha Trang,

Vietnam. Also remind them they are in international waters and this is a British flag plane and what are their intentions? Refuse to turn around."

Cat switched on the emergency frequency and listened to one of the Indian pilot's request they turn around and follow them. Cat pretended he couldn't hear them very well due to radio malfunction and repeated their destination was Nha Trang. Cat could almost reach out and touch them and held up his radio mike for the Typhoon pilot on the left to see and shook his head. They continued to fly in formation with them heading out to sea for another thirty minutes when they both saluted Cat and Trish and pealed off and turned back to India.

"Flight crew you were wonderful. We're home free and clear sailing to Nha Trang. Now are there any sandwiches and drink on board for your passenger? He whimsically asked, "and would Co-pilot Matthews like to join me?"

On cue Cat and Trish looked at each other again and then back to Atwater and both shook their heads laughing.

"Lling, this is Captain McCoy. Would you see if food and drink are available for our passenger and the rest of us? Miss Matthews would you assist Lling in serving our passenger," he said in the interphone.

Lling went back into the cargo bay to the insulated food locker followed by Atwater and Trish. They pulled down several of the fold up seats along the fuselage and sat down. Lling brought each a sandwich wrapped in wax paper and a bottle of soft drink and water and then went back up to the cockpit to keep Cat company.

"Miles, I know some game is going on here you're not telling us. It's pretty obvious you are more than you say you are. Clearly you are no banker. Who exactly is Miles Atwater," she said before biting into her ham sandwich.

149

"You are very perceptive Miss Matthews, but in our entire relationship these past few days you have seen me as I really am. I think I have seen you as you really are. What matters is the honesty we have shared in our conversations, two most memorable evenings back to back and another we'll share together this evening on our arrival in Nha Trang."

"How are you so sure I want to share anything with you?"

"It's because of this," he said reaching into his pocket and pulling out the Zippo lighter and showing it to her again. "I have held it to my ear several times these past days and asked Lt. Kincaid many questions about you and his answer is always the same…..he approves of you. Perhaps you would like to hold the lighter to your ear and hear it for yourself."

He held out the lighter to her. She looked at it for a moment, then to Atwater and reached for it and slowly brought it up to her ear as she continued to look him in the eyes.

"Yes, I do hear something. It's coming through now. Yes. Yes, of course Lt. Kincaid," she said handing the lighter back to Atwater without saying anything further and taking another bite of her sandwich. She purposely chewed very slowly.

"And what did he say?"

She swallowed and took a drink from her soda and looked over to Atwater.

"He advises me to wait until this evening and ask him my own questions about you before doing anything crazy. Guess we'll have to wait till later to get the truth out in the open."

"I see Miss Matthews. Honesty or Truth is it? Or is it honesty and truth? I guess you want it all."

"Something like that, Miles, would help me understand what's going on."

"Be careful what you ask for Trish as those two words are powerful, complex and both filled with shades of gray. I have been a student of those words for some time and still learn new things about them everyday. Each of those words represents something that must be used wisely. I do think the trait of honesty is more built in and truthfulness is more learned, however, you can define them as you like."

"So what is it Miles, are you more truthful or honest or both?"

"Trish, let's leave it this way. In the last three days I have known you I have been totally honest with you. Truthful? Yes in all the important matters that count between us so far. Totally truthful with you? No for valid reasons I hope you will respect for now. Sometimes knowing the truth demands we do something just, something righteous, something that answers the echoes across time to make things right. That's where your heart and head separate. Sometimes you have to listen to your heart. Sometimes you have to listen to your head. Sometimes you have to listen to both. Sometimes you must withhold the truth to get what you want. Sometimes withholding the truth prevents others from being hurt. See how complex this is?"

"What I see is you dodging my questions very skillfully."

"Trish, I just told you the truth that I haven't been totally truthful with you. Can we not leave it at that for now?

"Yes, you are right! Let's leave this alone for now. Now tell me about Nha Trang."

Atwater was glad to tell her about the city which the French referred to as their 'Riviera' on the South China Sea. Many wealthy French would winter there away from the cold European winters. He told her of its lush physical beauty including the most perfect white sandy beach in all Southeast Asia with water so clear and blue it would soothe your eyes

151

forever. Beach road, with its multicolored villas, was something to behold. He continued that the French had problems with the Communist insurgents, but all was quite under control. He talked about the people, the food and local customs and ended his conversation saying he had something special for her to see that evening. As he finished, Lling walked back and said to Trish that Cat would like a break for a sandwich and if you would come back to the cockpit. They were over half the way there and making excellent tailwind speed, as she relieved Cat. By the time Cat got back to the Cargo bay, Atwater was stretched out on the fuselage seats pretending to be napping with his hat over his face, but Cat knew he was busy thinking about something.

Chapter **27**

Lining up the '*Lucky Seven*' to land south to north with the South China Sea on the right glistening off the moonlight was a sight to behold for Trish. Atwater was pointing out the beach road and town of Nha Trang just ahead. Cat had called in to the tower and was instructed to land, turn around and stop until an escort car out to direct them to the tarmac. The bumble bee profile of the C-46 flared in to a perfect landing. As they were landing they could see the civilian airport building complete with rotating beacon and on the other side of the field French fighters, transports and helicopters. The escort jeep arrived and Cat let go the brakes and began following them. Instead of going to the commercial terminal, they were lead to the military side where ground personnel directed them to their parking spot. Atwater went into the cargo bay asking Lling to come with him. When Trish shut off the engines, after their 9 hour journey, it became instantly quiet. Both Cat and Trish relaxed in their seats for a moment saying nothing. The necessary paperwork complete, Cat and Trish walked back to the cargo bay which was full of civilian and French Military Police standing over the four well worn armored sacks. When they appeared the French MP motioned them to deplane. No climbing down the ladder as they had a regular mobile stairway staged for them to walk down. Standing at the cargo bay door Cat and Trish saw four police vehicles with lights flashing. Atwater and Lling were standing in front of several policemen, as well as several French MP's. They walked down the steps and then over to the group. No guns were displayed, but no one was laughing either. Even Atwater looked a little strained. He was speaking excellent French answering the police questions and showing them what appeared to be his passport. When he finished, he turned and stepped over to Cat, Trish and Lling.

"They want everyone's passport. Can you give them to me please? Seems everyone's been looking for us," he said with a grin.

Everyone reached into their pocket and handed their passport to Atwater who in turn handed them to a uniformed Vietnamese Police Officer. Another military staff car pulled up to the plane and out stepped another French Military Captain who walked up to the group and all saluted. He gathered them together and when finished the French MP's walked up to Atwater and spoke. Miles turned to Cat, Trish and Lling and said to 'follow me' as they walked over to the staff car Atwater saluted the French Captain and got into the back seat. Trish followed as did Cat. Lling got into the front seat. The French Captain then got into the back seat with them and pulled down the jump seat and faced them straight on saying nothing studying each persons face intensely in the dimly lit interior. He gave Trish a complete visual going over with a smile mumbling 'Mon chéri' and then moved his eyes over to Atwater and continued in a stare down with him. Cat and Trish were clueless on what this was all about and could only imagine the trouble they were in. The silence was deafening. The car began to move slowly and then picked up speed as it left the tarmac. Following them was a jeep with two French MP's.

"You've got yourself into a smoking mess now," he said in French flavored English and burst out in laughter as he reached over and shook Atwater's hand. "We glad to see your sorry face again."

Atwater simultaneously burst into laughter as Trish and Cat looked at them both confounded.

"Merci Capitaine Jadot. These are my friends, Pilot Cat McCoy and Co-pilot Trish Matthews and Engineer Lling behind you." He said pointing to each as Jadot shook their hands.

"I have been instructed to take you to the Colonel's Villa under house arrest. You'll be guarded until morning and taken to police headquarters for questioning at 10 am. The Scotland Yard boys are arriving later tonight to grill you in the morning." Jadot said, "When this is over I have an exquisite bottle of merlot to share with you and learn of your mischief."

"I look forward to that evening Jadot," he said as the car slowed and turned into a large villa Trish figured out was on Beach Road and just across the street from the South China Sea. The car stopped on the circular drive at the front door. The jeep with the French MP's was right behind. The driver ran opening all the doors for everyone to get out and stood at attention.

"Here you are. Have a restful evening. Staff inside will take good care of you prisoners," Jadot remarked and laughed again as he patted Atwater on the back. "Only restriction is you can not leave the house as the MP's will shoot you!"

He paused and looked poker face at Trish, Cat and Lling who froze in their steps.

"Just kidding. I love to pull your goat! Relax and enjoy the Colonel's Villa," he said with laughter in his voice as he got back into the back seat of the staff car and drove off. The two MP's stood 20 feet away with arms crossed as Atwater turned to his three bewildered companions who clearly were not smiling.

"My friends thank you for getting me here. Don't worry about Jadot, he is really a great guy and quite the joker. He really did get your goat! Tonight we will rest up and get ready for the police interrogation in the morning. After that you'll be off to Singapore. The housekeeper Mai will show you to your rooms and prepare a light supper for us in about 30 minutes. Please gather on the lanai near the pool for a cocktail with me."

Atwater led the group inside where Mai and two other house servants were waiting. He told her in French who everyone was and asked for separate rooms and the light supper to be served on the lanai. All were escorted to rooms outside past the lanai facing the large pool that shimmered invitingly in the dim electric lights. The pool and grounds were completely walled. Everyone walked into their rooms and one by one the doors closed.

Chapter **28**

Cat, Atwater and Lling were sitting in metal chairs with canvas seats around a large glass topped table being handed cool drinks by one of the servants while the electric fans on the ceiling slowly turned creating an enjoyable breeze. Trish had to shower and wash her hair and so enjoyed the heavenly lemon scented French milled soap she used. In her small travel bag she had one rolled up cotton dress and pair of sandals and decided that even though the dress was very wrinkled, it would have to do, as she didn't want to put her flight uniform and boots on again. She dried her hair the best she could and combed it back. Lipstick was all the makeup she put on. Looking at herself in the mirror with wrinkled dress and wet hair she smiled and said quietly, 'it is what it is.' She walked out of her room and toward the lanai where Cat and Atwater were engrossed in conversation. As she approached, they all stood and looked at her and then held a chair for her between them.

"Gentlemen, I apologize for the wrinkles and wet look, but had to change into something else," she said.

"In this Vietnamese Riviera paradise you can wear anything you want and look anyway you want. I think I speak for the table when I say you look marvelous," Atwater said smiling.

Trish did not blush this time, but accepted the compliment and said 'thanks' to her men and was served a glass of chardonnay. She pestered Atwater about explaining their treatment upon landing and how he knew Captain Jadot and who was this French Colonel? As Mai brought out their light supper consisting of French bread, sliced chicken, vegetables and salad, Atwater continued deflecting her questions good heartedly with questions and statements pointed right back to her and Cat. The entire episode was becoming comical and outright fun as Trish, Cat and Lling had to play his information stalemate game of not knowing what to expect next. After supper, and after several glasses of wine, all stood and clearly wanted to retire for the evening, except Atwater. He walked up to Trish who was standing looking into the beautiful tiled pool with cascading fountain burbling in the background.

"Trish I promised to show you something special this evening. Care to take a walk with an Aussie. You won't be disappointed?"

"You know I will Miles. Where too?"

"Follow me," he said as he held his arm out for her again and they walked towards the front door. Once outside and approaching the French MP's sitting in their jeep talking to one young woman on the wait staff, Atwater stepped forward and spoke to the Sargent who nodded back and then gave instructions to the Private sitting next to him. Atwater turned back to Trish and arm in arm they walked to the front gate and out across Beach Road, and across the beach to the shore. Behind them ten paces was the MP.

"Sorry about the chaperone, but we'll pay him no mind" he said as they strolled along the wet sand. Trish slipped off her sandals and walked into the gentle waves lapping the beach and feeling the cool water bathe her feet. They continued to walk along. Trish stepped on a rock and almost lost her footing, but Atwater was there to grab her arm. He then held her hand.

"Better let me hang on to you before you disappear into the South China Sea forever."

This was another first for Trish. She had never held a man's hand in her life and wasn't quite sure what it represented, but she was not protesting and even accepted it and after walking another 100 feet down the beach it became normal.

"Have you ever seen a more beautiful sight? The moon, the reflection of its rays off the water, the delightfully cool sea breeze. Do you think this is paradise Trish?"

"In the last three days we have known each other Miles, I am beginning to think you have something to do in creating paradise. I am just glad to be with you," she said.

Atwater pulled her close, and with the French MP looking on from a distance, kissed Trish as the waves lapped at their feet. The kiss lasted a long time and slowly they separated and resumed walking hand in hand along the beach. When the MP whistled at them, they knew they had to return to the villa so reversed course and walked slowly back across the sand to the Beach Road and then into the villa where Atwater thanked the MP's before going inside the front door with Trish. The house was quiet except for Mai who came out of the kitchen and greeted them. They continued out through the lanai and walked along the pool deck. When they got to Trish's room he said good night and gently kissed her. She went inside her room and closed the door falling back on it with a smile.

Chapter **29**

The 1949 French Army Peugeot 203 staff car gathered prisoners Cat, Trish, Lling and Atwater from the villa at 9 am Friday and drove them with MP escort to Nha Trang Police Headquarters on Tran Quang Khai Street. It was the beginning of a bright sunny day as they got out of the car and were escorted by the French MP's and then two more white shirt civilian police officers to a large conference type room with a large table surrounded by chairs on the second floor. The door closed behind them and the four were alone standing and looking around the room and out into a central court yard with lush vegetation. Minutes later the door opened and a plain clothes Nha Trang police officer entered the room followed by Inspector Barton Musk of the Singapore Police and Inspector David Hildebrand of Scotland Yard. They asked all four to set across the table from where they sat.

"I am Captain Trung Thieu of Nha Trang provincial police. We were notified by Singapore police, Scotland Yard, the Indian

Air Force and British Army to detain you for questioning in regards to a gold smuggling operation they all say you are involved with. Inspector Musk here would like to start the questioning of these suspicious circumstances," he said in very good English.

With all their passports in hand Musk opened them all and looked across the table comparing faces to names.

"Now I recognize two of the flight crew here. John McCoy and Trish Matthews from our visit on Tuesday. Now this must be Lling Munai the third member of the flight crew with the Malaysian passport. Miss Matthews, did anyone put a gun to your head on your journey to India and then here?"

"No."

"Was there anything unusual about your flight to India or here? Did anyone toss anything out of the plane or parachute to the ground?"

"Nothing unusual happened Inspector. We took two jeeps, some gas and four British Commandos to Poona, India, then flew here. No one pushed anything out of the plane in flight nor parachuted out.

"And you Captain McCoy. Do you agree with your co-pilots story?"

"Yes Sir. That's it. We flew the charter exactly as Mr. Atwater here ordered it," he said looking next to him where Atwater was seated.

"I see, which leaves this new person of interest. Tell me Richard Kincaid, are you the mastermind behind all this?" he said staring directly at Atwater as both Cat, Trish and Lling turned and stared at him too.

"I don't know what you are talking about Inspector," he said, "Can you clarify your question?"

"Mr. Kincaid have you been impersonating a banker named Miles Atwater of the Hong Kong and Shanghai Bank?"

"No, and for the strangest reason people keep calling me by that name, but I don't know why!"

"Did you charter a plane in the name of the Hong Kong and Shanghai Bank and fly to Poona, India with a load of gasoline, four British Army Commandos and two jeeps?"

"I chartered the plane, yes, and paid for it with a cashier's cheque drawn on the Hong Kong and Shanghai bank. I gave the owner of the charter service, Mr. Chen, the cheque and business card of Miles Atwater at the bank for him to call and verify the check was good. The cargo manifest included the gasoline and jeeps I bought in Singapore, but I know nothing of Army Commandos. I did carry four close personal friends to India for holiday, however, and they were dressed in army khaki uniforms."

"Now wait a minute Kincaid. I have here in a sworn statement of Larry Chen, owner of the MalSing Air Charter Service, that you visited his offices with a British officer, displayed a gold sovereign and said you were going on a rescue mission to India, and I quote, 'to get the Army's gold back for King and Country.' Do you remember saying any of that?

"Inspector, I told Mr. Chen a story of my brother's death in 1942 while on a secret mission to Malaysia and an account of gold missing from the Hong Kong and Shanghai Bank in Singapore that belonged to the Army at the same time, but there is no direct correlation between the two. I think Mr. Chen heard me wrong. I told him that for King and Country I wish that lost gold recovered and if he could find it, I am sure the King would give him a medal. It seems he misinterpreted what I said. I don't

163

think he understands the English language very well. I also showed him my lucky gold sovereign that reminds me everyday of my brother. Here is the receipt from the coin collector in Hong Kong for that 1938 coin. You know I had to pay 5 times market value to add that to my collection. Would you Inspectors like to see it? I carry it with me always," as he pulled it out of his pocket and placed it on the table along with the receipt."

Cat and Trish sat back listening intently to the question and answer session and clearly were enjoying the performance that Miles Atwater, who has turned into Richard Kincaid, was giving, or whatever his name was. Each of the inspectors looked at the receipt and coin and placed it back in front of Richard Kincaid.

"What were you doing in Singapore in the first place and who were those men that looked like Army Commandos?" Scotland Yard's Hildebrand asked.

"We all were attending the 10th anniversary reburial ceremony in the Pasir Panjang Military Cemetery in Singapore on Monday for our brothers that died mysteriously at the beginning of World War II; cut down in a Japanese ambush on the Kota Tinggi Trail in Malaysia. We decided to all get together on the tenth anniversary of their death as brothers of our brothers. Here is last Tuesday's issue of Singapore's *Straits Times* newspaper article of the ceremony along with pictures. We are all veterans and wore World War II uniforms out of respect for our fallen brothers," he said pulling the newspaper from his travel bag and opening it to the article and handing it to Hildebrand.

Hildebrand and Musk looked at the article together and became a little embarrassed and were beginning to think they were on a wild goose chase. The newspaper was passed around the table and when Trish and Cat looked at it they focused on the pictures and were surprised to see seven faces they knew intimately. Trish pointed to the face they knew as Jefferies and his man mechanic Beng. The picture was captioned,

> Attending the ten year re-burial ceremony in uniforms worn by their seven brothers who died together in 1942, were these seven younger brothers, also veterans - Richard Kincaid, brother of Lt. Gerald R. Kincaid (Australia); Peter McKnight brother of Private James McKnight (Australia); Kim Beng brother of Corporal Yo Beng (Malaysia); Craig Alsip brother of Private Kenneth Alsip (Australia); Alvin Perth brother of Private Lester Perth (Australia); C.V. Desai brother of Private Milind Desai (India); and William Standish brother of Sargent Thomas Standish (Great Brittan).

They glanced at each other as things were beginning to click into place, however, that didn't stop Inspector Musk from continuing the offensive.

"Why did you charter the plane and who do you work for," Musk asked.

"I work for myself in my company TOSA which stands for Trans Ocean Security Associates. I provide security and special services and am currently under contract with the French Government here in Indo China. The plane charter was partially paid by them to bring in a shipment of needed spare parts. The plane went to India to drop off the jeeps in Poona so my brother C.V. Desai could start a taxi business. I picked up the spare parts there."

With that last revelation, a bewildered Musk and Hildebrand stood up and walked out of the room for a private discussion leaving Richard Kincaid aka Miles Atwater sitting stone faced, silent with eyes forward at the table.

"Listen Musk, unless you can point to some illegal activity here with evidence that will hold in court we have nothing," Inspector Hildebrand of the Yard said, "unless you can tie this bunch to the 1942 missing gold."

"We have the impounded sacks they took off the plane. A Colonel Dusant should have those sacks downstairs by now. Let's bring them all down for a look see inside to settle this once and for all," Musk said as they both walked back into the interrogation room.

"We have the four sacks you brought from India downstairs in an Army truck. We will all go down to the truck to see if you have the British Army's gold."

Everyone got up and were led downstairs to a back parking area behind police headquarters where a French Army truck was parked, along with a staff car. Two soldiers were milling around the truck talking and smoking. Standing nearby in the shade was a French Army officer smoking a cigarette by himself. Richard Kincaid, Cat, Trish and Lling were led over to the back of the army truck and the soldiers lowered the tailgate with a bang. There were the four sacks sitting on the edge as the French Officer approached them from behind.

"Salut Lady and gentlemen," he said in excellent English as everyone turned around and faced him, "I

166

am Colonel Marcel Dusant of the French Army. Captain Kincaid delivered the spare parts we ordered him to find anywhere in the world yesterday and now you have suggested to me he is a smuggler and those sack contain contraband. This is preposterous and I request you release those sacks from police impound immediately."

Stepping forward to the Colonel, Inspector Musk introduced himself and said, "Colonel, we believe those sacks to contain gold stolen from the British Army in 1942. We are here to claim it and return it to the British Treasury. I ask that you open the sacks and reveal their content."

The Colonel looked over to the two soldiers and shouted in French an order. Each took a pick axe shovel from the holders on each side of the truck, came around to the back of the truck, motioned for the onlookers to step back and started hacking at the sacks until they split and chrome plated washers began spilling onto the ground. They continued hacking the two remaining sacks with similar results. Dripping off the truck into a pile on the ground were thousands of washers. Musk walked forward and held out his hand in the steam of washers and grabbed a fist full and threw them down.

The Nha Trang police captain was the first to laugh followed by inspector Hildebrand of Scotland Yard and then everyone erupted in laughter as Inspector Musk's face turned bright red in embarrassment. When the laughter died down the three policemen met and the Nha Trang police captain said to the group of four. "All charges dismissed. You are free to go. Our apologies for the inconvenience."

Cat walked over to Inspector Musk.

"Inspector, can I have my gold coin back," Cat asked, "That's very valuable you know."

Musk reached into his pocket, handed it back and walked away into the police headquarters shaking his head with Inspector Hildebrand and the Nha Trang Police Captain behind him. Richard Kincaid walked over to Colonel Dusant, stood at attention and saluted. Then they hugged each other smiling.

"Captain Kincaid, so nice to see you back. Sorry I couldn't greet you last night, but I had meetings in Saigon and flew up first thing this morning. I trust you had a good evening."

"Your hospitality was 'parfait.' Will you allow me to take you to dinner tonight?" he asked.

"Afraid not, you will be my guests again at the Villa with your friends this afternoon poolside and this evening for a dinner party. I want to hear all about your trip to Singapore for your brother's remembrance ceremony and meet that enchanting woman behind you Captain Jadot said was part of the flight crew. He will also attend dinner with his wife. Please introduce me to your friends and where may I drop you.

"At the plane please," as he turned and motioned for Cat, Trish and Lling to come over.

Introductions were made and they all climbed into his staff car for the short ride to the military side of the Nha Trang airport. They looked out the windows at the soldiers shoveling the sparkling chrome plated washers into the back of the military truck.

"Masterful plan Captain Kincaid. So glad I could help," Dusant said with a smile and twinkle in his eye. He repeated his invitation to use his villa this afternoon and again stay for dinner and the night as his guests, a request that Cat and Trish could not refuse. He then dropped them off at the '*Lucky Seven*' and drove away. It was close to noon.

Chapter **30**

Standing there on the tarmac Cat, Trish and Lling looked at Richard Kincaid, aka Miles Atwater without saying anything.

"Lling check out the plane from top to bottom and see what needs to be done for our flight home and take care of it," Cat said, "and Trish, please prepare a flight plan for return to Singapore in the morning while I figure out where the flight office is. I'll cable home as I'm sure Larry and Jasmine would like to know where we all are."

He walked away and Lling was already up on the wing checking the fuel and oil tanks. Trish walked over under the wing and pretended to be looking at something. Richard Kincaid followed and faced her as she tried to ignore him.

"I would like to start over and re-introduce myself. I am Richard Kincaid, but everyone calls me Dickey," he said holding out his right hand.

"How do I know you are who you say you are Mr. Kincaid or Mr. Atwater or Mr. Whoever?"

"Well, I'd show you my Aussie passport, but don't seem to have it on me right now. I guess we can continue our discussion from the plane yesterday on honesty and truth now. I would like to add that in this forth day of being around you I find I want to be around you even more. I am already looking forward to the fifth day."

"Miles, or Dickey, or Mr. Kincaid. See how ridiculous all this now is. I don't know what to believe anymore. I don't know who I am talking too. I don't know if I can believe you" as she walked quickly away leaving him standing there with his hand out and climbed up into the 'Lucky Seven' to prepare her flight plan paperwork. Cat returned from the flight office sometime later and sat next to her in the cargo bay jump seats and told her they were scheduled for a 7 am departure in the morning. He also said he sent the cable to the MalSing office that crew and plane are aok. He began to talk about Dickey Kincaid's revelations in the police interrogation offices, but she told him she didn't want to discuss anything further about him.

"Ok Trish, but he is truly an amazing man. Even with all the drama and unanswered questions we had before about him have fallen into place. He is an honorable man Trish! You can trust me on that from what I've seen."

"Now I have four words to sort out when it comes to Miles or Dickey. They are honesty, truth, believability and your new one honorable. Cat, somehow I don't think we have all the truth yet. There is still something missing here, but I think I can agree with you about the honorable word. What he did to gather those other men to remember their brother's death really moved me. Ok Cat, I'll give him a chance, who knows, he may have another name we'll be calling him this afternoon."

They wrapped up their paperwork, gathered their large flight travel bags with a change of clothes and climbed down the stairs to the tarmac. Lling was standing there and said he had to change the spark plugs on two engines and temporarily repair a couple of holes in the tail fabric torn in India and he would head into town tonight and see the sights if Cat had no objections.

"By all means Lling, have a good time tonight. We're off at 7 am so don't overdo it," he said as Dickey approached in a French Army jeep and stopped in front of them both.

"Miles and Dickey's taxi company at your service," he said with a smile which brought a smile and laugh from both Trish and Cat, "Where to or would you like me to give you a little tour of the town?"

Trish put her bag in the back and jumped in the front seat. Cat had Dickey's bag along and jumped into the back seat.

"You've been leading us around in circles for days. No need to stop now," Trish said as Dickey drove out of the airport and proceeded to give them a road tour of Nha Trang starting with the large Buddhist statue north of town and then proceeding past the train station and on into the downtown area teaming with people on bicycles and honking cars giving it a bustle of its own. They drove past the many shops, restaurants, bars and hotels lining the streets on a beautiful Friday afternoon. French soldiers were everywhere walking in groups to the next bar on their list. They proceeded south onto beach road, past Colonel Dusant's villa as Dickey Kincaid continued slowly down beach road. Dickey leaned over to Trish so she could hear.

"And over to my left my dear, don't you love the white sand and the blue water I promised you?" he said, "water so blue that it matches your eyes mon chéri."

"Dickey, if that's you real name, you're using your flattery thing again and it won't work any more, but I do like the view even though I don't like you," she said leaning over and giving him a kiss on the cheek.

He smiled and looked lovingly over at her and continued on to the end of the road where it forked to the hamlet of Binh Tan and the tidal inlet and turned around and headed back to the villa. He continued to expound on how beautiful it was here and the closest thing to paradise he has ever seen. Cat and Trish laughed at his jokes while taking in the sights and enjoying the warm breezy ride when they reached the villa and turned in and parked in front. Mai greeted them again, along with the same servants and they did a repeat from yesterday taking the same rooms. Mai served them a late lunch and everyone decided to go swimming at the beach to confirm the blueness of the water and whiteness of the sand. Mai found a blue swim suit for Trish after looking at her once and amazingly it fit. She also found some spare swim trunks for Cat and Dickey. They gathered up some towels, sunglasses and a picnic basket of drinks and headed across the street singing *Waltzing Matilda* with gusto and laughing when they became stumped to the next words. Blankets were spread out, a big beach umbrella rented and they raced into the blue water together from the white sand. Cat and Atwater soon found out that Trish was quite strong and fought hard as they tried to dunk her. She skillfully submerged and confounded them repeatedly as she repositioned herself for sneak attacks from behind them. After 30 minutes of enjoying the water all decided a rest on the beach was in order. After drying off and having a beverage, they lay down on their towels with Trish in the middle facing the opened umbrella. She didn't want to burn and asked Dickey if he wouldn't mind putting some lotion on her back. What should have only taken a few seconds he stretched to several minutes until she said jokingly she didn't ask for a massage.

"Dickey, will you tell us now the whole story of your brother and what all this is about? She asked. "And I want to be the first to congratulate you for that magnificent performance at Police headquarters."

"Ah we're back to the truth thing are we? Yes, I will tell the story. Remember after our dinner in India on Wednesday evening I told you the story of my brother's death. Well that was all true, but there was more I didn't tell you. The Army officers, who presented the flag to my parents, also presented the Zippo lighter they took from that Japanese officer named Ichido Yomeida in 1945 after the surrender. The lighter was the key and started the whole investigation as to my brother's death, whereabouts and circumstances. I had given that lighter to him for Christmas in 1941 and had it engraved with his name. I painted the Australian flag on the lid myself. Well my mother gave it to me as a keepsake and I have carried it with me every day since. There are echoes inside that lighter you know."

"There were a total of seven bodies in that mass grave they discovered as a result of Yomeida having that lighter. The Army forensic boys did a great job and identified everyone, but it took a long time. Finally, in December 1946, we had the official burial of the seven together in that Singapore Military Cemetery. I suggested the whole squad be buried together and so did my parents after thinking about it, and then we had to convince the other families involved in India, Brittan, Malaysia and at home in Australia. Through correspondence we found everyone's next of kin: widow, if they were married, children, and parents and got their consent. At the funeral ceremony I met the families and amazingly each had a son present, about my age. We all shared the loss of our older brothers in common. Well after the ceremony we all got together for a meal to get to know each

174

other better. Naturally, the younger brothers bonded immediately and realized that while we had each lost a brother to the war, we had each now gained six brothers in recompense. The hurt and pain we all felt individually was now shared and it lessened the mental load on all and eventually strengthened us. Now I have six other brothers."

Trish was finding it hard to hold back her tears and when Dickey noticed she was close to crying grabbed one of the spare towels and handed it to her to dry her tears. Cat was also moved by his story and felt more respect for this man that truly confirmed he was honorable and something of an inspiration.

"Sorry guys, I didn't want you to get emotional about this. It's just a story and you wanted the truth," he said.

"It's a beautiful story Dickey," Trish said as she stopped tearing up and looked at him in a new way.

"You are an amazing man Dickey. To assemble all the 'brothers' together for that ten year ceremony last Monday shows the kind of honorable man you are," Cat said. "however, a couple of things. Please explain the man we know as Jefferies, who chartered the 'Lucky Seven' before you and had us take four sacks to Poona and then jumped off the plane. What was in those sacks? And then you had us go to Poona and we brought four sacks back that contained washers instead of gold. Are you going to tell Trish and I what this is all about?"

"Ok, I'll tell you some of the story, but ask you both to understand that I can't reveal the whole story, as too much is at stake and those Scotland Yard boys will continue to snoop around. You know, loose lips sink ships. Things you don't know, can't cause any harm. Anyway, here goes. Jefferies, actually Craig Alsip, gave you some coins as souvenirs before he jumped. When I found out, I knew this was trouble as you would surely take them to the police. I see you only gave them one coin, which means you each have three. Is that not true?

"I must admit we each kept three coins and now I have a forth." Cat said.

"Yes, my three are in my suitcase in the apartment," Trish said looking at Dickey leaning on her elbows.

"Well we are all accomplices now in gold smuggling and in this together as I see it," he said with a smile and chuckle that also brought a smile to Trish and Cat. "Only difference between you folks and me is the degree. Anyway, I had to immediately put a backup plan into place fast, as I knew you two boy scouts would go the police in Singapore. It was just a lucky guess that you only turned in one coin to that Inspector Musk. I knew he would check out the coin and see it was the Army's missing gold from 1942. So, I chartered your plane and you know the rest. From the police viewpoint the gold is still missing, which is what we all wanted in the first place. They just have suspicious circumstances leading nowhere. Now there are other good things that came along with this adventure I put you through, and that was the opportunity to meet you Cat and your friend Jasmine. My great surprise and joy has been to meet someone special that is right next to me. Fate was at work here and I think I found something more precious than the gold."

"Dickey Miles, you know what I like about you? You never give up on that flattery thing and I admire you for that. If you come a little closer your golden girl will reward you," she said reaching over and planting a kiss on his cheek again and smiling at him.

They decided to go back to the villa and swim in the pool and gathered up everything and started walking across the sand to the villa. Trish held Dickey's hand the whole way back as they teased and joked about how cool he was with the police that morning and so sure of the outcome. All laughed at how embarrassed Inspector Musk was when the washers tumbled to the ground. After a swim they all returned to their rooms to get dressed for the Colonel's cocktail party.

Chapter **31**

Cat, Trish and Dickey all met up again on the lanai in whatever casual clothes they had brought along on the trip. It was just after 6 pm when Colonel Dusant walked to the lanai in his uniform.

"Hello again," Colonel Dusant said as Cat and Dickey rose to shake his hand, "Looks like you are all refreshed from a busy afternoon at the beach. Plenty of color in your faces. Here are your passports compliments of Inspector Musk. Let me get out of this monkey suit and join you for a drink. Won't take a minute. Jadot and my surprise should be here soon."

He walked away to his bedroom in the house and on the way told Mai to prepare a pitcher of vodka martini's, several bottles of wine and some of his favorite French camembert cheese and a tin of crackers and the chilled shrimp and cocktail sauce. As she was scampering to the kitchen, Jadot opened the front door and entered with his stunning wife Bridgette and her older sister

Nicole visiting from France to soak up the sun. All walked to the lanai. The Colonel appeared just behind them wearing white slacks and a colorful Hawaiian shirt and introductions were made all around. The servants appeared with the martini and wine glasses, followed by the wine bottles, pitchers and hors d'oeuvres. The evening then got off to a roaring start. Dickey's joyous task was explaining in French who everyone was and no one could believe Trish was a pilot by the way she looked. All couldn't wait to hear her story. Jadot talked about how his wife and her sister had come to see him, as they were only married two years and he hadn't seen Bridgette in over ten months. Bridgette told of her wild adventure trip halfway around the world to get to Nha Trang. The Colonel remarked how his wife went the other way to Paris for a month to visit her ailing mother and about the villa which was his fathers. He told how he came here many times for winter or summer holidays as a youth. It was only fate, luck and a little arm twisting that got him assigned to this sector of French Indo China.

Cat remained very sociable during all these exchanges and told some very funny stories about his year flying the 'hump' from Assam India to Kunming, China. At the same time he was only thinking of Jasmine and couldn't wait to take off in the morning and get back to Singapore. Dickey continued to translate and everyone was having fun listening to the story, translated into either French or English and then waiting for the reaction on everyone's face. Mostly there was laughter. Sometimes just an 'ah ha!' Back and forth this went on for an hour with the martini's and wine doing their best to keep things lively and entertaining. Finally it was time for Trish to tell her flying story starting in 1944. Dickey translated it perfectly after his second martini and especially the part where her mouth said 'yes' to being a stewardess again in Sydney, but the brain was saying 'kiss my ass.' This brought the house down in roaring laughter for the longest time. Dusant had quite the portable phonograph setup on a table inside the house and he decided to put some mood music on. He had quite a few jazz records, but mostly French popular and ballad artists, some classical, and dance band selections from several American musicians, including Glen Miller, Les Brown, and Hoagie Carmichael. It seems many in the world enjoyed Hoagie's famous song *Stardust*. Everyone got to select an album or song as the evening wore on. After a buffet dinner and several more bottles of wine Dusant was personally showing Nicole how the phonograph worked. He was so charming and smooth it was hard to believe he was a seasoned resistance fighter in World War. Cat, feeling a little awkward knew it was time for him to say goodnight and bid everyone goodnight and retire early. He told Trish they would leave at 6 am for the airport and she got the message. Dusant began to play more slow dance music and all of sudden there was *Stardust*, which reminded Dickey and Trish of their first dance at Raffles on Tuesday. He asked her to dance and they stepped under one of the lanai fans as the music drifted out to them. Jadot was also enjoying the song and joined them with Bridgette. Trish immediately saw how in love they were. Dickey held Trish comfortably close as they slowly swirled on the tile flooring. Then she looked straight at him.

"You know you haven't told me the whole truth about the gold. Isn't there a pirate's oath or something I can say that will let me know what's really behind all this?"

"Yes, there are two words you can say and my whole pirate's soul is yours."

"And what do I have to say?"

"I will," he said.

"That's an answer to a question. So what is your question Dickey?" she said baiting him along, but not very well prepared for his next words.

"I love you Trish and have since the moment I met you Tuesday night in the Raffles Long Bar. Don't you see, we are destined for each other? Fate has brought us together. Can you understand that? Can you believe that?"

Trish stopped dancing and asked to go over and sit on the ledge of the pool on some cushions. She took off her sandals and sat down and put her feet into the water pulling her summer dress up to keep it dry. Dickey took off his shoes, socks and rolled up his pants and sat beside her. He reached into his pocket and pulled out the Zippo lighter and handed it to her.

"Remember what you said," as Trish held the lighter to her ear smiling while pretending to be listening intently.

"Yes. Yes. I will wait and see. And yes," she said lowering the lighter cupping it in her hands.

"Before you ask I can't tell you what he said."

"Withholding the truth are we?"

"Yes, it's on a need to know basis and you don't need to know now."

"That's not fair Trish. You are leaving in the morning and I would like to know now!"

"Oh, a new word in our ever expanding dictionary is it? Fair, you want what's fair?

"What I want is for you and me to be together."

"Now you're overwhelming me Dickey in ways I can't explain. I think I know what your question might be and I asked your brother for guidance on responding to it. If I tell you what he just told me will you honor it?"

"You know I will."

"I asked him if you were the one for me and he said yes. I asked him if you were sincere in your feelings and he said yes. I asked him about the gold smuggling and he said that was complicated and for me to wait and see before making judgment, and finally I asked him if we need a cooling off period to catch our breath and he said yes. You give a girl a lot to think about Dickey Miles and I need time to think things over. Yes, I'll leave here in the morning. It's my job and I love flying more than I can express to you right now."

"I understand Trish. Look at the lighter again. Pull it apart and tell me what you see inside," as she pulled the lighter apart.

"I see nothing inside the case or on the lighter jacket except some scratches."

"Look closer. Those are not scratches, they are map coordinates."

Trish squinted in the dim electric lights to see, but turned to let the bright under water pool light help her make out what appeared to be map coordinates scratched on the jacket.

"I'll be darned. Are these the coordinates where your brother buried the gold?"

"Yes. He was on a mission to bury the Army's gold in Malaysia to keep it out of the hands of the Japanese and scratched the burial coordinates there, which I didn't really notice until last October. Since the Army had no record of my brother's mission and never explained why he or any of the other six men were there, we just let it go at that. At the time the Army either refused to tell us the truth, or really never knew themselves. The beginning of the war in Malaysia was very confusing and troops were getting killed everywhere by the Japanese, however, I had lingering suspicions that there must be more to this. I know there had to be a reason for an artillery officer to be there and concluded it was for his map reading skills. He scratched those coordinates to deliver them to who ever ordered the mission and it must have been someone way up in the British Army, who had vast authority and power. That person never got the coordinates. Trish, I got the truth from that lighter and it only made me more upset."

"What did you do next?"

"I can still only speculate how this all started, but know for certain the tragic ending of the gold squad I call the 'Un'*Lucky Seven*.' My brother and all those other wonderful young men died for gold. Our good friend Inspector Musk confirmed to you today that the missing gold was real. I hope I got him off the trail to continue thinking it is still missing, but he may continue the hunt."

"Dickey, how did you find the gold?"

"Oh, that's the easy part. My world atlas zeroed in to the general location and a survey map of Malaysia I bought in Singapore get me within 500 feet. I had traveled to Malaysia and met up with my new brother Kim Beng to do a little gold prospecting on the Kota Tinggi trail. I explained the situation and my plan for the gold to him and after some time, probing a large area with sharp metal rods, we narrowed our search to an abandoned grave yard and struck the gold sacks buried about a foot down between two graves. I was then standing in my brother's footsteps and began reliving what he was doing ten years earlier! After the military funeral cemetery this past Tuesday morning, we 'bothers' got together for a meeting where I revealed the truth about our brothers death, the gold and my plan to help them and everyone in their family. Alsip and Beng had already spirited the gold to India and raced back for the funeral ceremony. We all took the oath of silence as no one else needed to know the truth except us."

"You told me at Raffles that the gold came from the bank. How did you know that?"

"Well this took more research and eventually took us into the records of Lloyds of London. I used an insurance agent brother in Sydney, you know as Jefferies, to make inquires, and sure enough, in their loss ledgers for 1946 he found a payment to the Hong Kong and Shanghai Bank for the Singapore gold gone missing due to the Japanese invasion. This means the gold has been written off. The Bank had to pay the Army and filed an insurance claim with Lloyds, who paid them off. So the gold is finders keepers as far as I'm concerned. The insurance boys may be after me next, but there's nothing they can prove."

"So you found the gold and we rescued it last Saturday and flew it to India when Jefferies hijacked us."

"Yes."

"Why India"

"They worship gold there and certain 'interests' paid us a huge premium for it. And since its worth even more to collectors, they will make huge profits. Everybody wins."

"Who is everybody Dickey? I can tell you want to stop your story here. Where is the money?"

"Oh, the money. Are you sure you want the truth?

"If you don't tell me now, I will hold you under water until you do," she said in a serous tone.

"Well, this is complicated. Jefferies, I mean Craig Alsip, and I decided to recycle the money into insurance annuities that would pay everyone in the surviving families' payments for life.

We even have a scheme to pay proceeds from long lost life insurance policies the seven purchased just before they were killed, that will fund the annuities. And we are going to set up a trust for the benefit of all Singapore and Malaysia theatre of war veterans. Clever No?"

"Beyond belief Dickey," she said with tears in her eyes again.

"A couple more things. It's so important that the families, outside my new brothers, never know where the money came from. Remember how the truth can hurt and withholding it can be the right thing to do. Well this is key and now you are the eight who knows the whole truth and must safeguard it. None of the families can get their loved ones back. As I see it the gold has allowed some just reward for putting everyone through all this. Everyone will have as bright a future as money can buy. It's gold for good!"

"I understand completely."

"So Trish, the golden circle is complete. We will put all the net gold money, which is more that three times it's face value, back into the insurance and banking system. Look at it this way. We borrowed the gold. Sold it for a tidy profit and put it back into the bank and more. So at the end of the day Lloyds has been made whole, only they don't know they have. In fact they will get back three times the lost gold's value, when we're done. Not a bad return on investment I say, but my just reward is you mon chéri."

Trish looked at Dickey again with tears in her eyes, but these were tears of joy and love. She wanted to be kissed and Dickey obliged. She finally knew the kind of man he was. Pulling away she said.

"Can you help me up, my legs and feet are getting all pruney?" she asked.

Dickey helped her up, and looked around and they were alone. They embraced and kissed again for the longest time.

"I'll be here when you decide Trish. Don't make me come down to Singapore to kidnap you.

"I've already been hijacked twice this week. Why not add a kidnapping to make it complete." she said as they both laughed.

"Do you know Mr. Atwater Kincaid you're a pretty good kisser?

"And how would you know a good kisser from a bad one."

"Oh, that's a woman's secret."

"Oh here we go with the truth thing again," he said laughing.

"Goodnight Trish. I am missing you already."

She walked away into her room, closed the door and then fell back on it again with a growing smile on her face, just as she had the night before. Whatever they had after their four days together they had just sealed with a kiss.

"Goodnight and goodbye for now my Dickey Miles," she said quietly out loud.

Chapter **32**

It was just before 6 am and Trish was ready to go. She had packed, dressed in her flight khaki uniform with hair stuffed under her blue baseball cap, but as usual, it just refused to stay in. She left her room, headed past the pool and across the lanai to the front door wondering where everyone was. Mai was waiting and said goodbye to her and bowed as she opened the door. There standing next to the Peugeot staff car was Dickey and Cat talking with the Colonel. She looked in disbelief at Dickey again. He was dressed in a camouflage uniform as a French Foreign Legion Captain. As she approached everyone turned and wished her good morning looking at her every move. She returned the greeting, but continued to look at Dickey.

"Dickey, I think we've more to discuss here," she said laughing as everyone got into the car for the short ride to the Nha Trang Airport. "British Commando yesterday and French Foreign Legionnaire today are we? What will it be tomorrow?"

"It's on a need to know basis mon chéri and you don't need to know," he said smiling responding in his typical Aussie cool, sly manner with twinkle in his eye. Everyone in the car had a good laugh over his comment.

Cat and Trish thanked the Colonel for his hospitality and the wonderful party he gave last night and complimented him on his phonograph collection. Soon they reached the airport and the 'Lucky Seven' could be seen from the car glistening in the morning sun anxious to lift into the sky and get home. The car stopped and Cat and Trish and their bags were soon standing alone on the tarmac next to the plane. All had said their goodbyes in the car, but for Trish it didn't feel quite right. She was missing Dickey already. He waved out the window as they drove away. She waved back watching until the car was gone from view. Lling came up to them and said the plane was ready to go and handed Cat the weather and the plane maintenance report. Cat asked him if he had a good time last night in downtown Nha Trang. His response was only with a big 'thumbs up' and a smile. After Cat and Trish did a plane walk around, they all climbed up into the 'Lucky Seven'. Lling closed and locked the cargo bay man door. Cat and Trish took their seats and began the preflight checklist. French Air Force personnel helped them with the engine start and stood by and then directed them to the runway.

"Ok Trish, let's go. Three and one half hours and we're home," Cat said as they got clearance to take off and roared down the runway lifting off into another beautiful morning. The South China Sea was shimmering in the morning sunlight as they turned south heading down the coast past Hon Tre Island and then Cam Ranh Bay. "Leaving paradise is tough, but we did enjoy it for a while."

Trish did not respond and in true fashion choked down her emotions and focused 100% on her co-pilot duties in straight faced businesslike form. Dickey thoughts come up often with a smile, but they were quickly extinguished with the tasks at hand. They flew down the coast past Saigon, Can Tho then set course straight south for Singapore. The Malaysian coast appeared and they followed it down until Singapore appeared just ahead. The landing sequence for Changi Airfield went smoothly and as they taxied to the MalSing tarmac and hanger familiar faces were standing and waiting for them. Cat's eyes were only focused on Jasmine who was waving at him. The C-46 stopped and Trish killed the magnetos and the 'Lucky Seven' grew silent. Lling had the cargo door open by the time Cat and Trish walked back. They climbed down the ladder. Jasmine no longer cared what anyone thought and rushed up and began hugging Cat the minute he turned around as Trish and Larry Chen looked on smiling.

"My flyboy is home. Thank God you are safe," she said pulling away with a joyful smiling face and eyes a little teary. Cat was at first a little embarrassed, but didn't care anymore what anyone else thought either and hugged her again, this time giving her a kiss to a clapping Trish, Lling and Larry.

"Welcome home," Larry said shaking Cat, Trish and Lling's hand in his fashion. "Come to office and tell us what going on."

After turning in all the flight paperwork, Cat, Trish and Jasmine trooped into Larry Chen's office and sat down. Cat went through the entire story, saying there was no gold and never was any gold. He said Atwater just confused everyone into thinking there was gold for some scheme he had cooked up that he and Trish could never figure out. And the real news was that Atwater was really an Australian soldier of fortune named Richard Kincaid working for the French Army. Trish listened intently to Cat's made up story and nodded at the right moments to add credibility. They both knew much was at stake and Trish more than anything wanted to just make the whole thing go away, as far as Larry was concerned. With very little questioning, Larry said he was glad too this whole thing was over. He did smile and say that both charters were a profitable event, which was what he had his eye on. Jasmine listened, but wasn't buying the story as there were too many people chasing them for the tale to end as it did. She also knew when Cat was uncomfortable and every word out of his mouth made her more suspicious.

Cat invited Larry, Jasmine and Trish to dinner at a local Changi Road grill that evening, but Larry begged off with another 'previous engagement.' Jasmine said yes before he even finished speaking. Trish nodded and said 'fine' as she desperately needed to talk with her friends about Dickey. Cat and Trish said goodbye to Larry who gave them several days off as promised. Cat made arrangements to pick up Jasmine later at 6 pm and then went out to his Land Rover with Trish waiting in the front seat for the short drive to 963 Upper Changi Road and a little rest and relaxation before dinner.

Chapter **33**

Cat went to pick up Jasmine and then returned to the apartment for Trish for the short ride to the Starlight Grill. As she got into the back seat of the Rover Jasmine greeted her with an indescribable glowing smile on her face. She noticed Cat was unusually bubbly and cresting on his own catnip high. Something was up, but she couldn't put her finger on it, as her thoughts were only focused on her Dickey Miles.

They were seated outside on the patio at a table under a slowly turning fan that made the calm of the early evening more enjoyable. Their server came back with the three shaken vodka martinis with olives Cat ordered and placed one in front of each of them. Jasmine was dressed more alluring than Tuesday, if that was possible. Trish was dressed in another of her breezy, light colored buttoned dresses that still made you notice her, while Cat wore slacks and his own Hawaiian shirt. They all looked at each other and simultaneously reached for their glass by the stem, lifted them and after a clink all around, sips were on the way down to loosen up the tongues. Delectable Singaporean hors d'oeuvres filled the table and everyone dove in. When Jasmine asked about the phony story they told her father, Trish and Cat looked at each other and confirmed it was a lot of 'bull' to close the subject with him. Cat began telling the story from what he saw and knew, including explaining who the Miles Atwater she met really was and that everyone involved in both charters were really good guys on a mission for good. He told her about the seven brothers and the ceremonial cemetery service Dickey put together last Tuesday morning. He continued telling her that Trish and Dickey seemed to have something going on when Trish burst into tears, stood up and excused herself for a trip to the ladies room while holding a napkin to her eyes.

"What's going on with her Cat," Jasmine said.

"She's going through Dickey decompression. She's got the 'love bends' Jasmine. It all started this morning when she said goodbye to the one she finally fell in love with. I could be mistaken, but I think this is her first love!"

"No way Cat. She's 28 years old and as smooth, cool and professional as they come. Trish can handle anything."

"She's all that for sure, but our friend Atwater or Kincaid got under her skin."

"You may be right Cat. Love bends is it?" she said smiling and sipped her martini.

Trish came back to the table fully composed, sat down and apologized for her emotional behavior and confirmed she had feelings for Dickey Kincaid and for the first time in her life was unsure exactly what to do.

"What's wrong with me Jasmine? Why am I such a wreck after knowing this man only four days?"

"Love bends," Jasmine told her repeating what Cat said with a smile. "You are just decompressing from close contact with someone who has lit you on fire. Trust me when I say it happens, and it's a good thing. I know. Tell me Trish; is this your first serious relationship?"

"I don't know what it is. I've dated before. I don't think it is. How do you know what it is?"

"I think it is and it is very special what you are experiencing," Cat said. "I think you've put off everything for flying, when at the end of the day, it's just how we make a living, not our whole life. Dickey was just the key that opened up all the possibilities ahead of you in your life. You can re-bottle your emotions and everything will continue on as you call normal, or you can let some or all if it out and follow your heart."

"Dickey has forced me to think about things. Things I've hidden for so long for the joy of flying. I'm a little confused right now on what to do. I know he loves me, but I'm all fogged in. I keep swinging back and forth from never wanting to be away from him to denying we've had the most amazing four days together in my life. For God's sake he walked me down the isle a few steps in Wagholi, India. Remember Cat, me dressed in that beautiful red sari and he in his officer's uniform."

"Love bends," Cat said smiling, "sorry we didn't take a picture of you two love birds that night."

"Love bends for sure," Jasmine said. "No doubt about it!"

"He is smoking wonderful and I'm a smoking mess right now and still don't know what to do. You two are all I've got now to guide me. You seem so in love."

"We are in love and getting married. I asked Jasmine on the way here tonight and she said yes. We're going to tell Larry tomorrow," Cat said holding Jasmines hand, "and get married as soon as we can."

"That's so wonderful you two. Now I know why you two were glowing red hot in the Rover. I am so happy for you both wanting to spend your lives together," she said picking up her martini glass and toasting her friends. "You have made me feel so much better just by being with you."

Another martini round of drinks came and then dinner and the mood at the table soared with Trish back to her normal bubbly, feisty and witty best. They relived the four days with Jasmine listening intently and knowing they had all been on a roller coaster week physically, mentally and emotionally. After dinner they dropped Trish back at the apartment and Cat took Jasmine home. On the way they set several tentative dates for the wedding and agreed sooner was better than later. Jasmine immediately thought about her wedding dresses and where she would get them. Now all Cat had to do was finally face Larry Chen, but it all seemed anti-climatic. How could he say no, however, formalities were formalities. After several good night kisses at her front door. Cat headed the Rover back to 963 Upper Changi Road. He promised he would come back tomorrow afternoon to be with her and talk with Larry.

Chapter **34**

Cat woke up Sunday morning and found an envelope inside his front door on the floor with his name on it in Trish's handwriting. He opened it and began reading. She had caught an early morning commercial flight to Saigon and would catch an in country flight to Nha Trang to surprise Dickey. The closing part read:

> '....Cat, please thank Larry for me and tell him
> I am going back to Nha Trang to be with
> Dickey. Don't know how this will work out,
> but I can't stay in Singapore alone. Tell him I
> am sorry for the short notice, but will make it
> up to him somehow, someway, someday. I
> think you were right about the 'love bends!'
> Please send me an invitation to your wedding.
> We'll be there. Cheers. Trish'

Cat smiled and knew she had finally figured it all out for herself. Two martinis', a good cry and everything becomes crystal clear. He loved flying more than anything up until Jasmine. Trish was the same way until something made a change in her life and that was Dickey. The changes in everyone's lives this past week were incredible. From saying goodbye to Larson a week ago to asking Jasmine to marry him last night brought another smile to his face. Now all he had to do was talk with Larry.

"Piece of cake," he said to himself grinning.

Chapter **35**

Larry shook Cat's hand for almost a minute after he said yes to allow him to marry Jasmine. He was so happy he was almost giddy, but knew all along this was meant to be. Jasmine rushed up to her father after hearing him say that three letter word and practically knocked him over with a hug that was more like a tackle. That's how it started more than two months ago and it made him smile as he stood in the small Chapel anti-room of the Singapore Christian Chinese Church trying to straighten his tie.

"Here, let me help you with that young man," Larson Durant said, "brings back fond memories of my first wife and our wedding. Had the same trouble with my tie way back when."

"So glad you are here Larson to steady me out. I really appreciate you coming from London just for our special day today."

"Hey, a retired gentlemen has nothing but time on his hands. I want to thank you for providing the first class air transport. Those 'Super Connie's that BOAC have are a dream to fly in compared to the '*Lucky Seven*'."

"I wouldn't have it any other way my friend."

"When you wished that I could be your best man in the invitation, nothing could keep me away, except the airfare. When that ticket showed up at my flat a day later I can't tell you the joy I felt that you wanted me here more than anyone else on this planet to help you start a new phase in your life and one of the most important I might add."

Larson finished straightening Cat's tie and the two friends hugged for the last time. Larry Chen's brother Chow walked into the small room to join then as the other grooms men. All were joking and laughing waiting for the music to start, which was their queue to step to the alter. Jasmine didn't want a big ceremony and chose the small chapel that would only hold family and close friends. Cat's mother and father were sitting pretty much alone save for all of Cat's flying buddies and their wives. The Chen family and friends pretty much filled the place.

The music started. Cat, Larson and Chow appeared at the alter as Larry escorted his shining jewel Jasmine in the most lovely wedding dress she could find on a shopping trip to Hong Kong. In fact she had two. One white dress for this ceremony and a beautiful red dress she would change into for the Chinese flavored reception. Cat followed her eyes as she walked down the isle toward him until his keen peripheral vision noticed two familiar faces smiling and waving at him. It was Trish and Dickey. He smiled and nodded at them and then refocused only on Jasmine.

The ceremony went as planned, rings exchanged and the familiar 'I do's of two people in love echoed in the chapel. They walked down the isle arm in arm beaming and out into the courtyard sunshine, where a troop of Chinese lion dancers were waiting to bring good luck to the couple and ward off evil. The banging on the drums, firecrackers and colorful lions were enjoyed by all.

At the conclusion of the lion dance, Cat and Jasmine were whisked by limousine to their grand Chinese wedding reception in the Raffles Hotel ballroom where many other friends were waiting. After photographs, Jasmine changed into her red Chinese wedding dress and rejoined Cat in the reception line as everyone began arriving for the festivities. As the line passed the newlyweds, Cat accepted many red envelopes which he slipped into his jacket pocket. Finally, at the end of the line were two very familiar faces. Trish approached sporting a wedding ring and stunningly dressed. Dickey followed in his blue Miles Atwater suit. The friends shook hands and hugged. Jasmine and Trish then compared rings and had a good laugh.

"Oh, we just flew in to be with you on your wedding day as promised." Trish said. "We wouldn't miss this for anything."

"So glad you two could make our special day," Cat said, "Seems you've been busy yourself Mr. and Mrs. Kincaid. Trish Kincaid. That has a nice ring to it!

"Thanks Cat. We didn't invite anyone from our families. It was just an elopement. Very romantic and spur of the moment, but something we both wanted to do." Trish replied, "We flew back to India and were married in Wagholi at Dickey's brother Desai's house. I bought my own sari and we were married on the patio and had a wonderful celebration. I talked with your father Jasmine and he says you leave tomorrow morning for a surprise honeymoon with destination unknown until you get to the airport."

"Yes, father wanted it this way. He is such a man of mystery. He said we will be totally thrilled and will remember it for the rest of our lives. I guess tomorrow will tell the tale. I hope it's not back to Taiwan," as both couples laughed. Then Cat piped in.

"And what about you two lovebirds. Where did you honeymoon? In Bombay?"

"Oh we're still working on that honeymoon trip. Have been too busy with the business to take any time off," Trish replied.

"I see. Well, I wish you were coming with us on our mystery trip. We would have so much fun on a double honeymoon."

"Hey, never thought of that," Dickey said, "too bad we have to fly back to Saigon first thing tomorrow morning. Perhaps we can do something later."

Larry Chen walked up to the newly married couple from the ballroom which was rocking.

"You two need to dance first married dance. Come with me."

Larry grabbed them by the arm and ushered them into the ballroom as the applause grew louder as they reached the dance floor. There was a female singer in the band and as they stood there began singing a beautiful ballad by Jo Stafford named *You belong to me*. Everyone was standing around the dance floor clapping as Cat and his kitty swirled to the slow love song. The evening flew by and time for the newly weds to leave their grand reception party and head for their honeymoon suite on the top floor. As they approached the door, Cat picked up Jasmine and carried her across the threshold and slowly let her down and kissed the new Mrs. Cat as he kicked the door closed. The chilled Champagne waiting was opened. Two glasses were filled and the newly weds were finally and officially together and alone. The gentle clink of the glasses signaled they had finally made it.

"I love you Jasmine,"

"I love you too Cat!"

Chapter **36**

Cat and Jasmine began their first day together early with smiles and kisses as they had ended their previous night. They enjoyed being together more than ever and did not want to miss a thing. They were all packed and ready by 9 am to begin their mysterious honeymoon trip as the bellman knocked on the door to gather up their bags. They held hands as they followed him to the elevator and down to the lobby. Waiting for them was the limousine Larry Chen had arranged to take them to the airport. Bags loaded and they were off to learn their surprise destination. Sitting in the back seat holding hands they speculated where they would wind up that night, but not really caring as they discussed how mysterious and secretive her father was about the whole thing. While they were traveling in the general direction to the commercial terminal of the Changi airport the driver did not drive toward the departure area.

"Driver, where are we going? You missed the turnoff back there," Cat shouted.

"Mr. Chen said we stop at his hangar first. He has something for you."

They drove through the MalSing gates and headed for the hangar where they immediately noticed a polished DC-3 sitting on the tarmac next to the '*Lucky Seven*' with Larry Chen, Trish, Dickey, and Lling standing in front. Cat and Jasmine looked at each other and were beginning to realize a trick had been played on them. The driver stopped and opened the door and Cat and Jasmine got out to four smiling faces. They looked up on the side of the plane to see AIR MILES in dark blue letters painted on the side, with nose art depicting the word ZIPPO on the side with a lighter complete with Australian flag painted underneath it.

"Welcome to AIR MILES," Trish said laughing with Dickey holding her from behind around the waist and both smiling profusely. "We're all going to have our honeymoon together in Australia and enjoy the world's second most beautiful beach...Bondi beach. What do you say?"

"Do we have a choice you two?' Cat asked with a smile on his face as Jasmine looked on.

"Not really," Dickey responded as everyone broke out in laughter as he patted his hip pocket.

Jasmine and Trish hugged, and Cat and Dickey shook hands. Jasmine kissed her father and thanked him for the great surprise for their honeymoon. She told him it was already becoming unforgettable.

"Say Trish, who is that," Cat asked as a young man was walking around the DC-3, obviously performing his preflight checks.

"Oh, that's my new copilot Jacque. He is the younger brother of Captain Jadot. I am teaching him well and isn't he cute?" she said in her witty manner while kissing Dickey on the cheek.

"Trish you are amazing. What other little surprises have you in store for us?"

Dickey popped into the conversation. "We're going to island hop our way to Sydney. I want to show you some exotic places on the way. Don't know when we'll be back. Maybe never!"

Cat smiled and knew better about the man who had at least three plans going at all times. Not getting back was ok with him. Twice the woman married twice the man and it was going to work he said to himself as he looked over at Trish.

"Well what are we waiting for," Cat said as their bags were loaded on the DC-3 by Lling,

"One thing Trish. Are you going to tell me what all this 'Air Miles' stuff is about?"

"Captain McCoy, I'm afraid that information is on a need to know basis, and you don't need to know!" she said as everyone listening broke out into hilarious laughter.

Fade to Black.

STARDUST LYRICS

Songwriters: Hoagy Carmichael & Mitchell Parish

© 1929

Sometimes I wonder why I spend
The lonely nights dreaming of a song
The melody haunts my reverie
And I am once again with you

When our love was new
And each kiss an inspiration
Awe but that was long ago
Now my consolation is in the stardust of a song

Beside the garden wall when stars are bright
You are in my arms
The nightingale tells his fairy tale
Of paradise where roses grew

Though I dream in vain
In my heart it will remain
My stardust melody
The memory of love's refrain

RETURNING IN 2013

Stay tuned for the next action packed adventure of the *TOSA* files series featuring mastermind Australian Soldier of Fortune Dickey Kincaid, British flying bombshell Trish Matthews, American World War II pilot extraordinaire Cat McCoy, the sultry and mysterious Jasmine Chen, joker Capitaine Jadot of the French Foreign Legion and war hero Colonel Dusant of the French Army who will all return in;

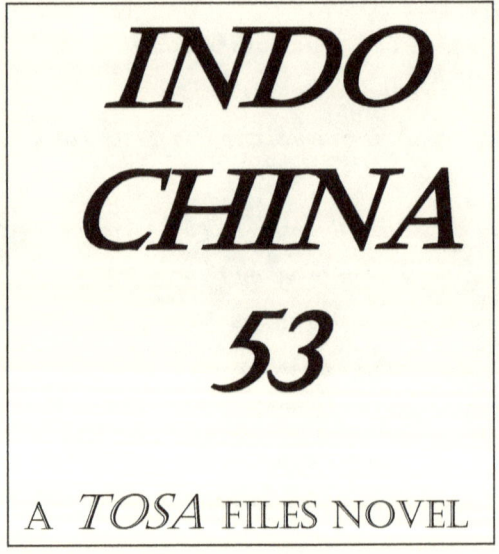

"Heads up....If we don't act fast.....everybody dies."

Another quality HEATHROW PUBLISHING book

www.heathrowpublishing.com

www.ingramcontent.com/pod-product-compliance
Lightning Source LLC
Chambersburg PA
CBHW020407150626
46554CB00012B/404